Teems is a great storyteller, and he transports the reader back to the Tudor era with great style.
—Washington Times, Review of *Tyndale: The Man Who Gave God An English Voice*

Teems pulls together a story of this enigmatic king with humor and pathos. Engrossing and entertaining . . . a delightful read in every way.
—Publisher's Weekly, Review of *Majestie: The King Behind The King James Bible*

To call it a biography is actually to conceal the brilliance of what Teems has achieved.
—Leland Ryken, Wheaton College, Review of *Tyndale*

Teems leads you inexorably into the depths and heights which often and unexpectedly surprise in their implication. It gives the reader an appetite.
—Tyndale Society (London), Review of *Tyndale*

I
RIDDE
MY SOULE *of*
THEE *at* LASTE

*The trewe accounte of Shakespere's secret commission in the creation
of His Majesties Olde & Newe Testaments & the amitie
between Wm. Shakespere & Sir Francis Bacon.
The final days of William Shakespere
including the account of his
cruelle and pitielesse
murder by friend
fellow poet
and rival
Master
Ben
Jon
son*

A NOVELLA

DAVID TEEMS

I RIDDE MY SOULE OF THEE AT LASTE

P. O. Box 682087
Franklin, TN 37068

I Ridde My Soule of Thee at Laste is a work of fiction. While the historical
props remain faithful to general scholarship—including names, titles,
chronology, reputation, and select passages of dialogue—the incidents
portrayed are fictional. Ancient biblical texts are presented in their original
spelling.

ISBN: 978-0-578-77016-1 (paperback)

Library of Congress Control Number: 2020918387

Printed in the United States of America.

Cover art: MAN OF WAR CREATIVE STUDIOS, Franklin, TN

Author web address: https://www.davidteems.com

For more information: info@davidteems.com

To the English language
and those who love it.

The poet is certainly the most unpoetical of all God's creatures.

—JOHN KEATS

This Marvelouslie Unexceptional Little Man

WHEN WE, THAT IS, WHEN I WAS A YOUNG BOY, I suffered an impediment, an irregularity in my speech apparatus that would not allow me to pronounce certain words—depending, of course, on the shape, dimension, texture, and viscosity of the word. I gargled, chewed, swallowed, or spit my English in those days. It came out gnawed, disfigured, comical, without soul or luster.

Buchanan tried to whip the devil out of me. "Find your tongue, lad!" Forgive this regression, but the man hated English. He may have hated everything by then, including me, but he was uncommon prickly when it came to English. You could tell by the way he bullied it. "Whoorish tongue," the old man cried. We did our best to mimic him note for note, gesture for gesture. He hated that, too. The verie whoore. Old Greek before Breakfast Latin before Scots himself.

The point is, what English I had was beaten or twisted into me.

We were orphaned and crowned before we could speak or take our first step. No father. No mother. Too many uncles. Hounds for baying. Buchanan was the most religious of my keepers, and the unkindest of spirits among them. We have been told the young queen of Scots was once his student, and that he loved her. Just before giving her over to wreckage, methinks. Pious frauds. Their wicked Jesus.

Then occasion smil'd.

We were thirteen. The affection of Esme Stuart was one thing, lavished, as it was, so liberally upon us, but the music of his voice was another. We were told he spoke our mother's French, the way it flutters about your neck like a small bird. But it was his English that moved us. For the first time, there was kindness in it, charity, heat and light. We didn't know language could do such things, that could charm with such violence, make such a disturbance in us. We empowered our cousin, gave him name, station, a new sense of gravity, height, and reach, all the toys of privilege.

Our French cousin was our excess, our vice, our great transgression according to some, treason according to others. They came one night and stole him from us, that is, from me. They tore me out of his arms, called me wanton. *Better that bairns should weepe*, they said. Barking curs.

We never saw our cousin again and were never the same after. But the charm was wound up. If we say we can taste words, we are not trying to be clever. And we are an insatiable king.

Try now, if you can, to understand the nature of our thoughts touching the translation, its want of a poet. We will consult with

Sir Francis. He is closer to the man, some say, than a brother. English is mistress between them. There, Bacon says, is empire. There, a great Britain.

> Where it is dull, where the ~~glow~~ ... gleam ... where the gleam of Majestie is absent or mute ...

When occasion smiles again, we will send for the man, Shakespere. Majestie has left its print on his art. After that hideous Scottish play, his best, darkest, and most complicated characters are ... us. Lear. Antony. Othello. Fools all. All.

> The ~~English~~ language must be the best that is in us ...

We are but names, titles, antiquities, forgotten speeches, an accident of blood and historical memory. Aye ... but this marvelously unexceptional little man.

No more of this.

By the unhappy title of this history we must, it seems, prepare ourselves for a tragedy. Some will escape. Some will not. For bully Ben Jonson can never suffer a true rival. He killed an actor once for botching his lines. Actors.

Southampton waits in our chambers. We will let him.

First, to our thoughts.

Then to our Lord of Southampton.

James R

 CHAPTER ONE

Unremarkable

EVENING WAS APPROACHING IN A SPECTACLE of mist and twilight that could not help but move even one as over-stimulated and surfeit-swelled as Henry Wriothesley. The earl had always muzzled his annoyance with the King and did his best to avoid him. But he could not refuse a royal summons. Following the usual ceremony and tedium of entering the palace, and having been directed to the royal bedchamber for some unknown business with His Majestie, he walked directly to the great window and stared out at the Thames. He always thought it the best view in the city. Idling, and a play still warm in him, he speaks the words quietly, with a scorn that seems to smile.

"This is the news: he fishes, drinks, and wastes
The lamps of night in revel; is not more man-like

Than Cleopatra; nor the queen of Ptolemy
More womanly than he . . ."[1]

At that moment, the King entered the chamber. "What say
ye, Harry?"

"Majestie." His flourish, a scented breeze, lithe and effortless.

"Come," the King says. "A speech of passion."

"There is a new play, Majestie."

"What is it called?"

"The Tragedy of Antony and Cleopatra."

The earl thought it best not to repeat the lines he had spoken
earlier. By habit, he has committed much of the play, as new as
it is, to memory. He continues to look out the window as he
speaks, transfixed by the muted sparkle of the Thames.

"I will tell you.
The barge she sat in, like a burnish'd throne,
Burn'd on the water: the poop was beaten gold;
Purple the sails, and so perfumed that
The winds were love-sick with them; the oars were silver,
Which to the tune of flutes kept stroke, and made
The water which they beat to follow faster,
As amorous of their strokes."

James had hoped to remain aggravated at the earl. The earl
continues.

"For her own person,
It beggar'd all description: she did lie
In her pavilion—cloth-of-gold of tissue—

O'er-picturing that Venus where we see
The fancy outwork nature: on each side her
Stood pretty dimpled boys, like smiling Cupids,
With divers-colour'd fans, whose wind did seem
To glow the delicate cheeks which they did cool,
And what they undid did."[2]

The words smile obscenely in the earl's mouth.

"There are such things, good, my cousin . . ." the King said. "Well, delightful isn't it?"

Wriothesley said nothing. For as long as anyone could remember there had always been small tension between Wriothesley and the King, undefined as it was. He understood the King's fondness for beautiful boys, and being one of them made him uncomfortable in spite of the unspoken pact of non-engagement between them.

And there was something about Southampton that made James recoil inwardly.

Henry Wriothesley had all the right friends, attended all the right functions, quoted all the right poets and playmakers. It was a token of achievement to have your lines tossed about by the Earl of Southampton. Whatever its source, he employed the line with a detached grace. Listening to Southampton speak was like watching him walk.

"Essex, God save all Christian souls, spoke of your poet too often for us to ignore his importance," the King said. "Even Cecil drops the great name on occasion."

"Cecil? Cecil is a mathematician. I had almost put the dwarf out of my mind." James did not laugh. "But Essex?" His words rise. "Essex was his Hamlet."

"Truly?"

"'The expectancy and fair rose of the state, the glass of fashion and the mould of form, the observed of all observers . . .'[3] Each line is a salute, a memorial to the glittering earl, hidden, as they are, so deliciously out in the open." The King suffered a small shudder of nerve, but recovered nicely, and undetected. "Unfortunately, Robert's sweet head was suspended on a pike before the play was ever performed. Which, I suppose, made it all the more attractive."

"A great mind gone bad," the King added.

"'That noble and most sovereign reason, like sweet bells jangled, out of tune and harsh; that unmatch'd form and feature of blown youth blasted with ecstasy . . .'[4] The old queen might have stopped the play altogether had she not played the heartsick lover, having extinguished the poor fool."

James thinks of his mother, the Queen of Scots.

"We have seen this play and did not make the association."

"Were you there when it opened you would have. The dead earl was on everyone's mind. He was the true ghost in the play. The queen was the poison in his ear." Southampton knew he had said too much but couldn't stop.

"Jangled a few of her sweet bells," the King said before he knew he had said it. Southampton started to laugh but didn't. A part of the royal idiom, it was a kind of treason (or very bad luck) to speak about the death of a monarch. "Wretched queen, adieu!"[5] the King added, to Southampton's relief.

The earl continued. "Will's father died earlier that year. The only medicine he had was words. And they poured out of him with muscle and spleen. He was at my house. HAMLET was a storm inside him," he said.

"The Christ that saved him," the King said in a quiet voice, to no one.

"Majestie?"

"We confess our amazement . . . cousin," the King said, "but surely the Hamlet you speak of is an exaggeration of the earl."

"Your Majestie judges wisely. Essex was a prop. We both know the earl didn't have the capacity of the Dane."

"Who does?" the King said under his breath.

"Prince Hamlet has the carriage of Essex, his bearing, the . . . the dash," the earl stuttered, "the flaunt, the charisma, his general high step."

"And the poisoned favor," the King interjected with a quiet solemnity. Southampton can play the adult on occasion, he thought, and be brilliant at it. He lamented the same to Cecil once.

"But that intellect . . ." The earl had a delicate way of making it sound like a question without the burden of a question mark. ". . . that peculiar command of English? These were beyond poor Robert. Would Your Majestie agree?" James nodded, vacantly. "Will used another prop," the earl concluded. "Someone closer to his heart."

"We can guess," the King said, ignoring the subtlety, "considering his amity with Sir Francis."

"Essex and Bacon were indeed the props, Majestie, toys of genius. Hamlet is both of them and neither of them." Wriothesley almost giggled. The King suddenly regretted that his former encounters with Southampton had not been as amicable.

Whether or not Southampton's assessment of the origin of Prince Hamlet was accurate or not, James had to concede the earl's evolved sense of these things, most specifically, the Poet.

Southampton had neither head nor stomach for Kingdom politics, at least not anymore, but he knew Shakespeare, and he knew the city. He understood the hum of its streets, who it fawned over and who it tired of, that it claimed its own nobility, crowned its own princes, ordained its own chief priests, acknowledged its own houses of worship.

"We regret we know so little of him." The King let the pentameter drag, like Cecil's foot, he thought quietly to himself, and not only think himself clever, but think it not slander to say so.

Years earlier, when the King first came to London, he was urged by Robert Cecil who was urged by his cousin Francis Bacon who was urged by his own good judgment to create the Lord Chamberlain's Men the King's Men. It was one of the first acts of the new reign.

"You would think him . . . royalty of sorts." Wriothesley watched for the cut of his words. Anticipating the earl's stealth, James was prepared. He remained quietly absorbed as the young Harry exulted in the merits of the Poet. "He and I have had somewhat of a departure . . . anyway, you summoned me, Majestie. How can I serve Thee?" His question was earnest. He didn't know what was behind the invitation, but doubted the King simply desired his company.

"We desired thy company," the King said. The earl smiled and bowed, and again with a delicate courtesy. He didn't believe a word the King said, but it was enough to have witnessed the transformation of the royal visage at the expense of a little hyperbole. He knew the King needed him for something, but said nothing more.

Wriothesley was little more than an amusement for the King, but proved himself useful nonetheless, more than the King expected. When speaking of the Poet or quoting a passage from one of his plays, cousin Henry didn't seem as empty-headed or as childish to the King.

James was aware, even if Wriothesley was not, just how close the foppish earl had come to losing his own head in the Essex debacle. Had his goodly mother not intervened with wailing supplication to the queen, his head would have been sheared off along with the Earl of Essex. But Wriothesley's head was not a political head. It was the head of a peacock—a rare shiny peacock, certainly, with name, title, and fashion sense, but a peacock. Essex was of a more dangerous stripe. Wriothesley was an ornament, a "pretty," as the queen once nouned her adjective toward him. And she thought it bad luck to kill a peacock.

The King was also aware there was some tension between Southampton and the Poet, though neither he, his First Minister Robert Cecil, nor anyone else seemed to know the source of that tension. To ask seemed wrong.

"We will call upon thee again," the King said. The earl understood this to mean some service would be asked.

"Adieu . . . Majestie." With a quiet bow the earl left the chamber.

"Southampton is of more use to us than we first thought," the King said to Cecil, who seemed to appear from nowhere.

"He will make some show of protest. He is no courier."

"The earl will do as we ask. It may sweeten the air between him and his beloved poet. Let us find out what the complaint is between them."

"Majestie," Cecil responded and walked away.

Queen Anne loved plays. It was her one relief, her one distraction other than childbearing or jewelry, from the seat she held in the kingdom and from the tension rising between her and James of late. London was a welcomed change from Edinburgh, but marriage to the King of England had become more of an office than a joy.

Arriving some months after the King, once she was settled in London, Anne was introduced to the playwright Ben Jonson and took an immediate liking to him. Perhaps it was his bulk, or his volume. There was something uncivilized about the man she could not articulate, a north-country crude she secretly thrilled at. With the exception perhaps of Sir Walter Raleigh, Jonson was as unlike the King as anyone in the kingdom. James hated Raleigh.

James indulged the queen, and at her insistence gave audience to Mr. Jonson. It was one way of maintaining peace at home. But the King would find a way to profit by it. Ben Jonson knew Shakespeare in ways Southampton did not. And his commentary would not be dressed in so much lace.

"The queen commends you most strenuously," the King said upon introduction.

"Then I am most strenuously honored, Majestie." Jonson made a flourish and with such slavish formality and ceremony the King's mind began to wander. Once upright, Jonson was forced to wait out the distraction.

"She is quite taken with your masques. Her heart is become . . . light. This does us great service." He wanted to say that it made life with her more bearable but didn't.

"Her Majestie is much too kind." The playwright made another flourish, and with even greater formality and greater ceremony. Upon initiation of the gesture, the King spoke softly to himself, though his words, like his gaze, pointed in no real direction.

"*Raram facit misturam cum sapienta forma*," he said. [Beauty and wisdom are rarely found together.] Jonson, at the nether end of his bow, laughed softly but audibly. The King wasn't sure what to make of it.

"Petronius had a tampering wit, Majestie." Jonson knew his Latin.

"Ben," the King said, with an obscene chuckle. Surprise was not an easy thing to extract from this king. The bullish Jonson felt not only the good fortune to have small audience with the King of England, even if it was just to please the wife, but the King addressed him by his Christian name.

"*Nam et ipsa scientia potestas est*," the playwright said. [Knowledge is power.]

"Sir Francis never wore a crown." The King knew his Bacon. But he was not in the mood for a discourse on power, in Latin or any other language. James was an anointed king at thirteen months old. There were few alive who understood power the way he did. It was the only parent he was to have. Jonson said nothing. The King shifted his weight and said distractedly, "Upon the queen's arrival in London, we indulged Her Majestie with a play. It pleased her not." Jonson smiled inwardly.

"May I ask the name of the play, Majestie?"

"We truly don't remember. Some silly business about a duke who turned over the rule of his dukedom to a noble youth who proved an unworthy substitute and bawd." He paused as an opinion mounted. "A scoundrel, actually. But to his credit, the duke proved himself a wise father to his possession." The play simmered in the royal head for quite some time after seeing it.

"We have seen many plays by this playwright, and while we can't say it was one of his best, in spite of Her Majestie's disapproval there was something marvelous about it, a rare delicacy in the lines, without weight or . . ."

The King's words stopped to allow him to float dreamily for a long breath or two.

Jonson's bristle didn't show. He knew the play. He knew all the plays. He certainly knew the playwright. Obsession being the dark occupation it is, he had studied the Poet's work, and with disturbing vigilance. He hid his aggravation.

Jonson was aware that the Poet had fashioned the play as he did many of his current plays, with the King in mind, including its title. But the King had judged correctly. After a run of fine tragedies, MEASURE FOR MEASURE was a disappointment even to Jonson. Jonson started to deny knowledge of the play, but suspected the King was too well informed.

"I know the play, Majestie. And am acquainted with its author."

"You laugh."

"May your Majestie have such memories." He let the pause expand between them. "We were all thrown together in the beginning—the two Toms, Dekker and Kyd, Kit Marlowe, Will Shakespeare, and me. There were others. We had to spew the plays out in those days, and at a pace that could hardly catch up with itself or render much that was any good. The muse is hopelessly monogamous. She's like the dog that way."

"What's that?" The King appealed to the pedant in Ben Jonson, though he wasn't impressed with his metaphors.

"In the early days," Jonson continued, "when the demand for new plays was out of control they were written by committee.

We didn't know any better. Thank God we were young. A motley brood of actors and wordwrights, we assembled parts together, primarily from the classics—Ovid, Plautus, Homer—all in the hope that a single story of interest might survive the confusion. Some wrote fight scenes because they were good with a sword. Others had a fist for the romantic line, some for the delicacies of court, and so on. The plays were awful, put together more by arithmetic than craft. The stitching was never very even." A single expulsion of breath that could have been laughter. "Forgive my presumption, Majestie, but a universe created by committee would be a very different place. According to the scripture, creation itself was set to order by a single voice, at the expense of one clear sentence, the prelude to all existence: *Dixitque Deus fiat lux et facta est lux.*"[6]

"Is not that same scripture written by scores of writers?"

"Contributors, indeed, Majestie, but to an aggregate of works, a compilation, a collection of individual books assigned and indexed by divine ordinance perhaps, but individual works nonetheless." The King nodded. Jonson continued. "We were the young lions, the new Homers, but for our craft to survive we had to abandon the community effort. Kit Marlowe broke away first. God, I miss him. What a snarl of talent. An animal. Will worshipped him." Something like surprise on the royal face.

"Come live with me and be my love, and we will all the pleasures prove." The King's recitation of Marlowe was without flaw, to the joy of the playwright. The King stopped, then looked at Jonson with a kind of pleasant vacancy. Jonson was moved not only by the King's retention but by his willingness to perform. "And, the rest . . . la ti ta ti ta ti ta ti ta." The playwright beamed.

"Marlowe has a way of getting stuck in our head. Especially in four and four, which we prefer over four and three. Though we know the five-beat line is the arithmetic these days. But that's neither here nor there. We did see a performance of EDWARD II at Whitehall." He stood mute, without an opinion about the play. "But tell me more about Master Shakespeare."

"The older he got the more indifferent he became toward the jig, that ridiculous spectacle at the close of a play. Though, in truth, he is proficient at it. He has quite the leg . . . or did once. He's become rather portly." Jonson laughed again. "He's done well, considering."

"Considering?"

"He is not a well-educated man, Majestie."

"All the more reason to applaud him, would you not agree?"

The King may wear a codpiece with room enough to smuggle a potted plant, he may have more tongue than mouth to keep it in, he may never bathe, but his intellect was not to be trifled with. And the King leaned favorably toward the Poet.

"He has an old head, you might say. And a magnificent ear."

"He is musical?"

"That is not exactly what I meant, Majestie, but in truth, he is. He plays the lute, or did once. I never heard him play but I have been told he had a lovely touch. And could sing like an angel. It was the lute, he told me once, that first taught him to put words together."

"I suppose we should be grateful to the lute, grant it knighthood perhaps," the King said, hoping the jest might prosper. Against all the good will and easy laughter between them, the King could not help but detect a mild contempt behind Jonson's words.

"Will is pretty closed about his past."

"Men of humble birth often are." The King took Jonson's hand and observed the brand on his thumb.[7] "Perhaps we all have histories we wish to keep silent," he said. "But please, tell us how he came to London."

It was clear to Jonson that the King was not inquiring about the Poet for the sake of conversation. There was some operation behind it, perhaps a royal commission, that is, another accolade for the Poet.

Jonson told the King what little he knew about Shakespeare's Stratford beginnings—his father's trade as a glover and sometime wool merchant, the local politics, even the lineage, the connective tissue between the Ardens and the Shakespeares. Coming out of his own mouth he realized how ordinary it was. He had little need to color his report with any smear of resentment however slight or undetectable.

"But what of the man himself?"

"He is glorious unremarkable." He meant it, and might have said those very words, but didn't. "He is honest, Majestie," he said, "of an open and free nature. There is precious little bigotry in the man or hard opinion about much of anything at all, and there is certainly more in him to be praised than pardoned." These words were rehearsed. The King was sure of it.

"Pardoned? For . . ."

"His insufferable excess. His wit is in his power. Would the rule of it were, too."

"Poetry is an excess of a kind, is it not?"

"I remember the players often mentioned, as if it were a commendable thing, that in whatever he wrote 'he never blotted out a line.' They said it with such . . . piety. I would he had blotted a thousand. Which I said to them, and they thought it malicious talk, when in truth, it was not."

"He says too much?"

"I do love the man, Majestie, our . . . honey-tongued Shakespeare. But he flows with such lack of moderation and restraint, sometimes it is necessary that he . . ." He realized he was in a passion, that his words had lost their gentility. And they *were* rehearsed.

"We have heard no such objection to the man," the King interrupted. "Though we admit his HAMLET is a trial." It felt good to laugh.

Mindful of his time and obligations, the King had no more ear for Master Jonson.

"He is possessed of excellent instinct, Majestie," Jonson continued, angling for more dialogue. "Musical instinct. I don't think he would be the writer London brags of without the lute in his foreground." Jonson's honest regard for the Poet was attractive to the King. It salvaged the King's good opinion, having almost soured. And Jonson's resentment was easier to take than Wriothesley's praise.

"Honey-tongued," the King repeated vacantly.

The King wanted nothing from Jonson but a true opinion. Having one, the conversation was over. The flourish Jonson made mimicked the movement of one of the bears at Southwark. Jonson stared at the floor beneath him and listened to the odd misshapen percussion of the King's departure.

"Indeed, Majestie," he said with cool menace and to no one but himself. "It is necessary . . . that he be stopped."

As he rose and turned, Robert Cecil was standing behind him.

"Lord Robert," the playwright said.

Cecil turned and walked away.

CHAPTER TWO

A Marvelous Wicked Talent

By MANDATE OF THE CROWN, and as it should be for blood this high and this blue, there is to be no less than twenty horns. It is the music he loves most—trumpets and cornets, the brass of exclamation, the entrance of Majestie, that is, himself. The air about the old banqueting hall is charged with royal effluence.

He is queenless for the afternoon. But he has been solo often since his arrival in London, a habit that will grow old with him. Also, the merriment that follows his Anne, the mirth she seems to arouse, and the attention she pilfers from the colorless king, makes her absence a welcomed event. He considers her devotion to the theatre excessive, "womanish." Even so, he has acquired a noticeable passion for plays himself, though he does his best to keep the knowledge of it contained.

Years earlier, in the first summer of his reign, at the London house of Southampton on the Strand, a revival of the two HENRY IV plays was arranged to lift the King's progress-worn spirits. It was strongly felt by the Master of the Revels, Edmund Tylney, that these particular plays, the two HENRYs, wildly popular in their time, would be a suitable introduction as well for the new monarch to the London theater. Cecil agreed, thinking it might help soften the labor of transition between the royal households.

The King was, indeed, entertained by the plays, but not as they had assumed. Everyone was certain he would fall prey to the smutty charm of Sir John Falstaff, but the fat knight left him "wanting," as he confided later to Cecil. He was entertained. He even laughed. But it was a mild amusement. Nothing more. The two plays were about kings, after all. Having been one since before he could walk, the whole notion of kings and kingship, the divinity of the crown, was an old preoccupation of his.

The twice HENRYs were about an old order giving way to a new one, an aging and diseased state succeeded by a state of promise, a subtle feature few but James would even notice. He was tormented all his adult life by the dream of succession, the rights of blood, the dues of birth. It made him old before his time. He was the Lord's anointed, with all the earthly pedigrees and all the validations of heaven. James was certain even the humblest of playgoers understood this basic truth of modern life.

While the King laughed at Robert Armin's portrayal of the fat knight, and while it did bring him much needed refreshment from the rigors of his progress to London, he never understood the former queen's fascination with Falstaff. He concluded that her tastes, unlike his own, were common.

A few refills of the royal goblet may have loosened the threads a bit, for James came undone at Hal's merciless lambaste of Sir John.

> ... there is a devil haunts thee in the likeness of an old fat man; a tun of man is thy companion. Why dost thou converse with that trunk of humours, that bolting-hutch of beastliness, that swollen parcel of dropsies, that huge bombard of sack, that stuffed cloak-bag of guts, that roasted Manningtree ox with the pudding in his belly ...[8]

Smut and oath may have been an Elizabethan art form, but it was especially appealing to a Scot. Even then, James concluded that this English playwright had a "marvelous wicked talent." Still, regaining his composure, he told himself that Hal was an exaggeration, a theatrical invention bred of a fine wit perhaps, but a mockery to the historic Prince of Wales.

The young actor who played Francis the tavern boy he thought quite beautiful.

As the play ended, even Robert Cecil noticed the hook in the royal mouth. Cecil nursed an ambivalence toward the playwright. Shakespeare had been the trophy poet of the Essex entourage, from whom Cecil only took abuse. And the affection the Poet eventually maintained in the heart of Cecil's cousin, Francis Bacon, was also to be considered. He was always congenial with Cecil, even mannerly, on whatever occasion happened to bring them together. Cecil might have been inclined to like the Poet, if only as one might pity a lamb prepared for feasting.

Now, years later, 1608 to be exact, at Whitehall, the King is to see another performance by the King's Men. Each step the King took as he entered the hall beneath the canopy of state was heavy with pomp, as ungainly as those steps were. The music did not cease until he was seated.

The ambassadors accompanying him on this occasion sat on stools below him, as everything was below him, as everything must be below him. The rest of them sat on benches. Of course, no one sat until the King was seated. Looking toward the stage, then looking around the hall, he spoke to Cecil indirectly, as if talking to himself.

"A turd for this hall," the King observed. Small laughter followed on cue from those sitting nearby. The King was in his rouse, having consumed a considerable quantity of French wine before entering the hall. "And the name of this play?"

"THE TRAGEDY OF OTHELLO THE MOOR OF VENICE."

"We do love a good tragedy," the King said with distraction. Cecil understood the Queen favored a comedy or a romance. Whether office holders, ambassadors, noble sycophants, spies, or other oddities of court, they had all acquired a taste for the stage, or admitted as much in deference to the royal whim.

With the attendance of each successive performance of the King's Men, James became more openly excitable. Smitten from the first lines of this new play, upon hearing the name Iago his calculations were swift.

A form of *Iacobus*, the King's own name, *honest* Iago, the *bold* Iago, the *good* Iago dominated the play, and with the cunning of a Cecil. Looking rather benign at first, even comical, Iago was the principal bad boy and archdeviant, the serpent in

Othello's Eden, the Machiavellian First Minister of the doomed and lesser-brained Moor.

Cecil steamed inwardly at Iago, though his countenance remained tranquil.

The King wasn't sure whether to be outraged or flattered. In the end he was delighted, which Cecil marveled at. The King knew he was in the power of the author, a thing that both frightened and exhilarated him. The charmed in the eye of the charmer.

The playmaker's audacity to take liberties with the royal name, however disguised it might have been, and to ascribe it to a villain, was a boldness only the covering of genius might hide. But the balance fell to flattery, as it so often did. The King felt an immediate and almost idolatrous attraction to the Poet, which unsettled him. "Not the one-half has been told me," he thought to himself.

In the back of the hall stood Ben Jonson watching the play, watching the King, watching the play, watching the King, watching the King watching the play. His heart rose with every grimace, every droop of the royal countenance, every sleepy nod. It sank with every smile, every hypnotic fixation, every spasm of thick laughter.

A pall settled over the room. The final words of the play were spoken with such a passion of loss and foiled justice no one knew quite what to do. The bewitched king looked about the hall, taking note of the effect, reading faces, how magisterial the silence. There was no jig, no dance, none of the usual revels to douse the tragic light that glowed in a kind of wordless epilogue.

The sudden ignition of applause and shouting voices resonated over the room and filled His Majestie's thoughts with something inexpressible. He rose from his seat, and everyone rose with him. It took some time for the noise to fade.

Looking over the press, James noticed Ben Jonson standing at the back of the hall. He bent forward and whispered something to Robert Cecil. Cecil, in turn, whispered something to one of his own guards. The guard walked over to Mr. Jonson and whispered something to him. Saying nothing, the playwright followed the guard through the small gathering toward the royal canopy.

"Majestie." Ben made his flourish.

"What think ye of the play?"

"Your players are the best in the realm, Majestie. I thought the villain rather fun, too."

"You're a sly wit, Master Jonson. You are eluding us. The play. Did it please thee?"

"Did it please?" The King smiled. It was a bold game to play in his presence. The King had already sampled Jonson's acid regard for the Poet. He said nothing, in the hope of a reply. "Yes, Majestie, it doth please me well. As a fellow of the craft, I have much to observe, and much to learn at the attendance of most any play. I do miss the poet's dancing, though."

"There is teeth in this answer, Ben."

Jonson hesitated a long moment or so before responding. "Please do not mistake my criticism of his work for small regard." The King nodded his head negligibly. Jonson continued, "THE MOOR is from an old Italian collection, and . . ."

"Cinthio," the King interrupted with annoyance. "Indeed, but the playwright hid his theft, and gave the original a second life, one we are sure it never enjoyed so . . . robustly."

"He has a gift for that, Majestie, for borrowing, enhancing, ascending a ladder another carpenter has made." Not wishing to further indulge Jonson's hauteur, the King came quickly to his point.

"We would meet the man himself, the man Shakespeare. Will you do us the honor of an introduction?"

Jonson made another flourish to the King, his mind full with sudden and steaming contradictions. "Majestie," he said. The King suspended any more discussion, turning as he did to Cecil for some private business.

A partition was erected as part of the stage, jutting out from its margins, a kind of scaffold overlaid with thick crimson fabric, designed and built by Cuthbert Burbage, the actor's older brother and set maker. Behind this partition, hidden from general view, the actors were going through their usual post-performance buzz. The Poet was speaking with Robert Armin, his Iago, when Jonson approached.

"The more I study the script, the more flexible it seems."

"Meaning?"

"Meaning I can do it like we rehearsed, the way we just played it . . . or I could do it straight, Will, take the jest out of it, make Iago a real devil, a real kissing Judas, not the clown. You certainly gave him the words for it." Armin had seen Shakespeare himself do a serious version of Shylock once.

At that moment, Ben Jonson approached the two men.

"Ben!" the Poet cried joyfully.

"Will."

"And what did you think of my Othello, my unfortunate Moor?"

"*Fu gia in Venezia un Moro.*[9] You know better than to ask me that, Will." A look of concentration fell on the thick pudding face. "I'm always obliged to give answer." Jonson had a way of trooping indelicately about, particularly with wordplay. You always knew where he was in the room. Shakespeare was about to change the subject, when Jonson continued, with emphasis. "However . . . since you asked. It was bloody awful, a real steaming pile, Will. No wonder Burbage hid his face in all that black grime. I would have, too. He might have put a sack over his head. Your game is fallen, old man, and from a great pissing height." The young jester, Armin, still standing by, could only gaze at the man of heft, and in stone amazement. The Poet's lately rounding belly rippled with such irrevocable mirth, it took minutes to gather speech. Armin grimaced at the two playwrights and walked away.

"Will, someone wants to meet you."

"Someone of note?"

"The King."

"It has been some time. We haven't seen so much as his backsides."

"Yes, Cecil is with him, too." Their laughter was that of schoolboys.

"Let us not keep His Majestie waiting." He made a mock flourish to his friend.

The two playwrights made their way from behind the partition to the royal canopy. Jonson was dressed in his usual black and carried more presence than the unassuming Shakespeare. But he always did. Where Jonson was bullish and peremptory, Shakespeare was finesse and understatement. Where Jonson was loud, Shakespeare was articulate. The two men, both actors, both assuming the role, walked with increased gravity the closer they came to the King.

Remaining seated, the King and Cecil were discussing the wrecking of the old banqueting hall and its future possibilities when the two men approached. The King was immediately aware of the Poet yet continued his discourse with Cecil if only to look less aroused with emotion than he was. In truth, the King was nervous, a sentiment uncommon for his station, though not uncommon with this king. His usual drained and court-worn appearance made good camouflage for this newly risen passion.

The Poet had grown plump, having lost his youthful and once goodly shape to middle age. What remained of his hair was long and well-trimmed, and his clothes were of an obvious fine tailoring. Still, his mien was nondescript. He made a rather middling presence for so large a name. Weighing nearly eighteen stone, Jonson was the dominant of the two—his image louder, his form a purer bulk. Even so, the King's attentions were fixed on the lesser figure.

Observing protocol, the Poet's eyes dropped a reverential height from the King's gaze. The King was not sure what he expected, but being the very fashion, the mirror by which nobility and commons alike checked themselves, being the sole index from which the fashion-mongers pilfered their latest clichés and parlorspeak, being the one poet elevated above all others in the realm, he may have expected something else, unsure, as he was, what something else might have actually been.

The King was two years younger than the poet, had lived a life of privilege, but looked older. They stood about the same height, though, in truth, had the King's body been a bit straighter or the plumb of his legs a little truer, he may have proven the taller of the two. When they at last fell into each other's gaze, some recognition passed between them, touched with a delicate, mutual, and, if not unexpected awe. The wary and moon-faced Jonson, standing at such close proximity, could do nothing but suffer the injury.

The King noticed the sincerity in Jonson's voice when he made the introduction. The change in tone was attractive, even sincere, elevating the moment. Shakespeare made flourish to the King's Majestie, not without a small groan of displeasure. Jonson wanted to laugh but did not.

The Poet suddenly grew in stature. Jonson was invisible.

"The man himself." As he said these words, the King descended from his seat to where the Poet stood. "Master Shakespeare, walk with us." The Poet smiled, though with little volume, and the two of them walked away, the King's guard following a few paces behind. Jonson remained with Cecil, his face dull, expressionless. Cecil read the wounded playwright with a delight of his own.

"Let us talk awhile," Cecil said. He wanted to add, "and find medicines for our grief," but didn't. The injured man and his little Iago.

"We commend your sense of court parlance, Master Shakespeare," the King said.

"Majestie."

"The grace with which you clothe the idiom does it great justice." Unlike most who come into the presence of majestie for the first time, the Poet was not anxious. "You write knowingly of kings. The first plays ever I saw performed in London were your HENRY IV plays. 'Then happy low, lie down. Uneasy lies

the head that wears a crown.'"[10] The King said the line with no
hesitation or search in his voice. "We must admit; we did not
know what to make of your Hal at first. We thought his prodi-
gality a little . . . extreme. For one of his blood, of course. His
society with such wastrel jacks as Falstaff is difficult to reconcile,
faithless as it is to the actual history. But . . . as you so skillfully
wrote, it made his transformation that much more of a delight.
Tragic his reign was so brief."

"Indeed, Majestie." The Poet wanted nothing more than to
fill the pause with text but left it to the King's pleasure.

"Southampton quotes you incessantly. You have filled his
heart with song, sir." With a hesitation, he continued, "If you
could only do something about the accuracy of the notes. He
butchers your best lines. Though he impales them on the knife
of sincerity. In spite of his feathers, he is somewhat tone deaf,
more cock than lark." He looked at the Poet with a slip of mirth.
The Poet grinned widely, amazed at the dexterity by which the
King crowded his metaphors. The King's own laughter was the
cackle and snort of a tavern wench. He knew the King was exag-
gerating Southampton's faults. "But he holds you in the highest
esteem, Master Shakespeare. For all his foppish drivel, he seems
to know of what he speaks."

The Poet found His Majestie most likable. He made no response as the King went on, not so much as a nod. His history
with Southampton, and the distance he now keeps from him
was not at issue here. "We will request your HENRY THE FIFTH
at Hampton Court in the spring . . . after Lent, of course. We
love Whitehall, but your plays, even as your name, have grown to
such dimension we must sue venues more agreeable. Anyway, the
plague has sent us packing, and out we must again." The actual

thickness of the royal tongue matched by the Scottish broadcloth it was smothered in made his English difficult to understand. "It is an inconvenience. Mister Tylney will see that your troupe is sufficiently financed and accoutered for your flight as well."

They walked slowly about the entire circumference of the room, the King content to carry the conversation on his own. It was his way. In passion or in the threat of passion, he talks, and talks, disclosing his thoughts indiscriminately at times, enjoying, as doubtless he always does, the sound of his own voice.

The Poet remained quietly amused and wondered somewhat at his own serenity and self-possession. He had known Elizabeth. She was great, but she was not "greatly good," as he put it. Her administration threatened ruin upon his father. Always wary of her, he felt a kind of suppression under her rule, one he did not suffer under James. HAMLET alone liberated him from the power of her spell.

Elizabeth was the only woman who could make the Poet nervous, except perhaps for Lady Bacon, his good friend's mother. Her wit was clean, the edges sharp, polished, like the blade that took the head of Essex. She carried a man's weight in terror. Being a woman, and more specifically, a woman in a world ruled and ordered by men, she had to work harder, rise earlier, be smarter, more dangerous, more subtle, take more counsel, lie more convincingly, make spectacle more spectacular. Anthony Bacon spoke of Shakespeare in the same manner; that being a poet of limited education and humble birth in a world ruled and ordered by a more privileged class, he too had to work harder, rise earlier, be smarter, and so on.

But enough of that.

What stood out most conspicuously in these moments was

the warmth of the King, inclined as it was toward the Poet. It was neither a pretended nor strategic warmth but an authentic one, seasoned with grace. All the calumny and ill reports the Poet had heard of his new sovereign were misinformed.

Because of a bout with childhood rickets and other trouble in his legs, without the use of a cane, a staff, or some human prop, the King was known to wander in the wrong direction. Or worse, he might amble into a wall or careen with some disgrace down a flight of stairs. He was much inclined, therefore, to lean upon whomever was near. A poet of rank is no exception.

Though the King wore fragrance to camouflage an inescapable funk, it wasn't working as well as he or the Poet had hoped. The herbs and sprigs of lavender did not help either. The proximity of the King's body against the Poet's, his hand upon the forearm, was soft and submissive. The smell added a measure of recognizable humanity, though unlike royalty.

"We will talk again," the King said. "Soon."

"Majestie," the Poet responded.

"Lord Robert will make the arrangements. We have something of weight we wish to discuss with thee. Speak of it to no one."

"Majestie." He felt foolish for the repetition.

"Until then," the King said. He turned to walk away while the Poet was in mid-flourish, an act that was becoming more of an effort. His doublet pinched.

CHAPTER THREE

Whose Song Could Outorpheus Orpheus

THE POET HEARD THE GREAT NAME OFTEN. Ben Jonson told him once that when Francis Bacon spoke, the greatest fear of those around him was not some harsh judgment of the law, but that he might stop. A "Daniel" he called him. They could not cough, relieve themselves, or even turn their heads, he said, without loss. "No man ever spake more neatly," Jonson said, "more pressly, more weightily, or suffered less emptiness, less idleness, in what he uttered." Jonson's purpose in saying these things to the Poet was not exactly a friendly one, though, once again, it did not have the effect he intended.

In summer of 1595, at the invitation of the Earl of Pembroke, Shakespeare was able to observe Francis Bacon for himself in a court of law (Gray's Inn). It was a warm day. The room was crowded beyond capacity, as it always was when Francis Bacon had the floor. No one made a sound when he spoke, lest the spell break. Ben Jonson was often guilty of exaggeration, but his account of Francis Bacon was precise.

They met, the Poet and the Philosopher, and found a gentle, true, immediate, and fond magnetism between them. The introduction was less eventful than we might assume, as it often is when great spirits meet.

Continually broke and ever frustrated in his attempts to gain employment and fortune in Elizabeth's court, against his mother's severest wishes, and against the high rant she excelled in and exercised upon him with a much spirited why-can't-you-be-more-like-your-brother hostility, Francis Bacon spent time at the theaters along with others of his feather, the rich froth of London youth, the very cream.

Francis found himself among a dash of young earls—Henry Wriothesley (Earl of Southampton), William Herbert (Earl of Pembroke), and the chief sparkle among them, step-son to the queen's then dead Robert Dudley, Robert Devereaux, the Second Earl of Essex, the pride of the age, a young man, who at the time, replaced the dead Dudley as the queen's favorite. Essex was the flame around which the noble youth buzzed and tacked about. He was, as was all his pack, quite taken with the Poet. Fashion demanded it.

Francis Bacon heard many reports of the budding new playwright, not only from his brother Anthony but from Anthony's friend, Christopher Marlowe. Always suspect of the herd, particularly in matters of art, Francis thought little of it. But at least on one occasion, the Philosopher had the opportunity to defend the Poet's honor, and long before he had even met him.

In 1592, Will Shakespeare had written only a few plays and one long and delicious poem. But few recognize genius better than genius, even when it's green. Bacon's admiration for Shakespeare may have had its beginnings one evening at the Tabard Inn in Southwark, and Shakespeare wasn't even there.

Francis Bacon had long learned the pulleys, levers, and geometric vantages of language. As a philosopher, a student of human thought and expression, he could not deny his fascination with a riddle as lovely as the one surrounding Shakespeare. Few at the time cared anything about his origins (he was not yet the great man). As far as anyone was concerned, the Poet had no origin before his first character came to life on stage. He had no father before Sir John Falstaff, no mother before Rosalind, no lover before the ripening Juliet, no prince before his Henry the Fifth. "Talent of this consequence," as Bacon was heard describing it, "is greater than its nativity, greater than the fortunes of its birth." Other than a few malcontent fellow playwrights, including though not exclusively Ben Jonson, curiosities or debates concerning the Poet's origins just never came up.

There were exceptions.

Robert Greene, a man gaunt in both body and judgment, a man of wounded insight, and yet of no small education, a man of thin red beard, a sometime playwright and pamphleteer, was dying a slow agonizing death of drink, diseased pride, syphilis, and other excesses of London tavern life. In spite of these impediments, Greene still managed to publish a piece of scorn called A GROATS WORTH OF WIT BOUGHT WITH A MILLION

OF REPENTANCE: DESCRIBING THE FOLLIES OF YOUTH, THE FALSEHOOD OF MAKESHIFTE FLATTERERS, THE MISERIE OF THE NEGLIGENT, AND MISCHIEFES OF DECEIVING COURTEZANS.

In a stream of bombast and vitriol, the author, as inflated as the title of his little work, referred to the young actor-play-wright-poet Will Shakespeare as an "upstart crow beautified with our feathers." *Our*, in Greene's rant, being a reference to the university *wits*, as they were called, his tribe. Greene denounced the young playwright as a poseur who dared to think he could "bombast out a blank verse as well as the best of you."

It didn't take, of course, and the syphilitic Greene didn't live long enough to see the Poet's feathers become even more "beautified."

That's an ill phrase, a vile phrase, 'beautified' is a vile phrase.

One evening, not long before his death, Greene was at the Tabard Inn, tipped heavily with quantities of sack, as was his custom. He was railing loudly, and upon a particular theme that seemed to abuse him fiendishly. Not unlike Jonson, he had developed a scorching obsession for Shakespeare.

"S'blood! No more of his whining Adonis. 'She red and hot . . . he red for shame but frosty in desire.' Jesu!" he added, guzzling more drink.

"Frosty indeed!" cried a woman's voice from somewhere in the tavern, inspiring a rhyme extempore. "Wag, wag that piddling little wick, which by my troth is more dead than quick."

Bellies of riotous laughter detonated throughout the tavern.

"How they gird at me," Greene responded. "See how the little worm offends."

"Sooth, sooth! Little scamp!" cried the same loud female voice. And more loud laughter at Greene's expense. The alcohol seemed to insulate him from the abuse, but he would not abandon his theme.

"On my life!" he protested loudly.

"What's left of it," a stray voice uttered quietly.

"Fie! Fie! A shopkeeper's son," Greene scoffed.

The besotted Greene waited for his words, which he thought came out rather nicely, to take effect.

Francis Bacon was at a nearby table with his brother Anthony. Anthony was in town on a rare visit from some business in France. Sitting with them was Anthony's good friend, the playwright, Christopher Marlowe. The Bacon brothers never had much use for Robert Greene. Anthony thought Greene's plays at best inanimate. Francis thought him of a good useful mind, but despised the deliberate waste of it, how he kept it saturated with drink.

Marlowe, who was known to use his own verbal whip on occasion, deferred the present encounter to his friend Francis. And with expectation. He knew what was coming, and welcomed it. Some of his better lines had been pilfered from Bacon's tavern rhetoric.

"There is a gleam of sport in thine eye, Francis," Marlowe said, playing the provocateur.

"Look at him!" Anthony said. "The poor sod is so eaten with the pox, there's little left of him worth disputing. Let him bleat. He's harmless."

"Then again," added Marlowe, "What is drink without a show?"

To the delight of his companions, and if but to watch him work, in the midst of Greene's polemic, Francis stood up solemnly, drink in hand. He addressed Greene and the delegation around him loudly but not disagreeably, gaining the attention of the room, saying, "Gentles all . . . if I may?" With that, and with a drunken nod of resignation, Greene ended his invective. The noise in the room at its usual volume during Greene's rant, abated quickly in anticipation.

"Master Greene, I speak for all present," Bacon said. "We are indebted to your wit, sir. Your plays are . . . divinity itself." Wild riot rose swiftly in Marlowe. "And your tracts, how dull and ill-informed a world in absence of them." He looked around the room. "I lift my cup and a grateful soul . . . in homage." (O-MAHZH, as he pronounced it.) He made a flourish then lifted his cup to the astonished Greene, as many of them began to do. Anthony Bacon, Marlowe, and others who had begun to drift along the rising current lifted their cups high above their heads as well, and then took a long draft as Greene looked on, stunned, silent, of a sudden unsure of the tribute.

Anthony leaned over toward Marlowe. "You'd think he was being crowned with the bays," he said.

Francis, tipped a few degrees with drink himself, smiling contentedly, in the voice and accelerated pace he often took in a court of law, continued.

"But concerning the poet you demean, sir, and with such flower, do you not overlook the holy gospels? Is it not written that the Son of Man was born in a stable . . . of parents humble, of possession lean, of means sparing, that at birth he lay in a lowly feed trough, a hay-strewn shambles rank with urine and camel droppings, that he came not in glory but in humility? Was not she who suckled him but a poor maid? Did not very kings of the East come and worship him? Did not the angels exalt him at his birth? Did heaven not riot with song? Did not the Christ himself, in his nonage, live as a poor carpenter's son, under a carpenter's roof, apprentice at a carpenter's trade, and break bread at a table made with a carpenter's hands?" His words were all speed and acuity, and each one plucked out of the air extempore. "Did the Messiah, the savior of the world, own the clothes he wore? And yet . . . did he not have the command of heaven in his speech, a voice that made the deeps tremble, that gave sight to the blind, that put song in the mouth of the dumb?" No one dared to move or speak.

Greene opened his mouth but Bacon raised his palm in protest.

"Tarry, sir, I fear there is more."

Francis held the moment in his power—not just for the effect of which he was master, but to gather himself from the drink of which he was not.

Marlowe whispered to Anthony, "I wasn't aware Francis had ever met Will."

"He hasn't."

"Consider the Twelve," Francis continued. "Were they not unschooled men, simples, mechanicals, men who labored not in their minds, but in their hands? Were they not lowly fishermen? Did they not smell of sweat, grime, and all the reeky emblems of their trade?" The pause was deft, the silence imperial. "But I arrive at the soul of my speech."

In the pause, you could hear the sound of Greene's labored breathing and little else.

"After spending time in the presence of their master, did these men not say things beyond the former reaches of their wit? Did they not amaze their mothers and their fathers, if they had them? Their wives, if . . . well. Like the prophet Isaias, their tongues were touched with coals of fire, their words with the divine. Does God mock us in this paradox? Does he not choose the weak to confound the mighty? Does he seek *our* approval? Are we so arrogant to test his appointments? Do we, like Job, lift up our voice with protest and interrogation to God himself? And Israel, were they not his own people? Were they not chosen of all the peoples of the earth, despised of all nations as they were? Do we question that which is in his power to give?" Bacon halted, but Greene was not disposed to speak, having lost his tongue and his stomach. At this, Francis approached the man gravely, and spoke his next words directly to his face, with great speed, pounce, and exacting rhythm.

"Was not David, the sweet singer, the gentle poet-prophet-prince, whose song could out Orpheus Orpheus, was he not left in the fields to tend his father's sheep when Samuel came to anoint a son of Jesse as Israel's king? Were his brothers not taller, stronger? Were they not men of greater state and presence than the boy in the sheep pens? I tell you, Master Greene, Samuel did not sit until the least of them was brought before him. The least, I say, the youngest, which by law and the courtesy of nations had little or no promise of estate, but by the election of a higher court. Was he not ruddy and withal of beautiful countenance, of fine shape, goodly to look upon? Was he not pleasing to the eye, his mother's favorite, and a virtuous? Did not the Lord say to Samuel, 'Arise, anoint him, for this . . . this is he?'"

Following another dramatic suspension, he whispered into Greene's ear, though loud enough to be heard by those present, for the room was stone.

"*Caeca invidia est.*" [Envy is blind.] He slowly stepped away from the stricken Greene, only to turn back and whisper again, fully sober, and in sterling English, "She should be dumb as well."

By habit and with his usual courtroom elan, Francis let his words suspend as in midair, that meaning might congeal in the poor man's ear. He then brought his appeal to a thundering epilogue. His words sped along with heat.

"O, ye of little faith! Ye of abundant, copious, express, and decisive little wit!"

Bereft of speech and courage, and having little stomach against the intellectual brawn of Francis Bacon, Greene stood up, and not without difficulty. Bacon did not hesitate, but continued his declamation.

"Despair not, Infortunatus!" He looked about the room. "The name of Master Robert Greene will live in perpetuity." He turned again to the smitten lamb. "In the umbrage, in the great shadow . . . of your upstart crow!"

Greene, flushed with drink and rage, his eyes aflame with blood and rheum, gathered himself to leave, to the rowdy sound of applause. "Raise your cups, gentlemen!" Bacon cried loudly, with the flourish of drink on his lips, as Greene bolted out. He shouted after the man, "See, Master Greene! How the giddy multitude do adore thee!"

It was brutal, merciless. Marlowe, not easy to amuse, was senseless with mirth. Anthony farted with the force of his laughter. It was the best entertainment Robert Greene had ever afforded a London audience.

 CHAPTER FOUR

Not a Poet Among Them

CONVERSATION WAS NEVER DULL. From their first impulses toward one another, Francis Bacon began to write essays not in response to Montaigne's rising popularity as it was assumed, but to calm the violent intellectual arousal he suffered in response to a line from a play, a sonnet, or some other subtlety of genius from his beloved friend, William Shakespeare.

The Poet fascinated the Philosopher like no one else in the kingdom. Upon seeing OTHELLO for the first time, Bacon, in one feverish sitting, wrote his essay "On Love." "Speak of me as I am," said the Poet's unfortunate Moor, "nothing extenuate, nor set down aught in malice: then must you speak of one that loved not wisely but too well." The Philosopher struck back epigrammatically.

It is impossible to love, and to be wise.

The Philosopher suffered appetite only the Poet could satisfy.

It is only fair to add that the Poet was just as wonderstruck with the Philosopher. In 1597, Bacon wrote an essay called "Wisdom For a Man's Self." "Be so true to thyself," he wrote, "as thou be not false to others." To elbow him into laughter, his poet friend put a variation of those same words in the mouth of a prating old fool.

> This above all: to thine ownself be true,
> And it must follow, as the night the day,
> Thou canst not then be false to any man.

The pentameter was the one rule the Poet bound himself to, even against the occasional aria that he never denied himself. But where the Poet fused lyric with meaning, the step with the word, his Philosopher friend did not. Bacon cared little for the music of a line. He thought it a distraction. Warning against the affectionate use of eloquence, he thought more of "things" than words. "More to the matter," he argued. Of course, with the Poet's usual stealth, the line resurfaced again in HAMLET. And from the mouth an impatient queen.[11]

Bacon laughed, and loved his friend more dearly for the jest.

It was necessary for Francis to maintain a distance, or at least the appearance of distance, from the playhouses. It was an unspoken rule for all men of breeding. But like so many things, it proved a difficult restriction to observe. Men of breeding crossed many boundaries. It was only proper to keep the appearance of such a rule, even if you had no intention of observing it.

Though he tried to limit his play going to royal or noble

venues, Francis Bacon found himself in the gallery a bit more often than he would like to think. No one really cared; they were all there, including quite a few men of breeding. He understood and admired his gentle friend at a level others were incapable of. The playhouse, or more specifically its premier playwright, was sustenance, the meat he secretly fed upon. There was only one mind capable of such a push. The paradox that surrounded Shakespeare was too appetizing for an evolved intellect like Francis Bacon's to ignore. Like most of them, Francis found little that was out of the ordinary about the Poet's exterior—a pleasing look, an agreeable countenance, a goodly shape (though the shape was losing much of its goodliness of late).

Francis Bacon stood just inside the entrance of the privy chamber. The King held a small book in his hand, rapt in what appeared to be thought.

"Francis, what do you make of this?" A game he was long acquainted with, Francis knew that if the King asked such a question, the royal defense was prepared beforehand. A dog of law, he had a nose for such things. The Latin was abused, but not beyond recognition. "*Ars est celare artem.*" [It is art to conceal art.]

"Art is art's grandest illusion, Majestie," Bacon said. He spoke with a hush disdain for his words as if it were a nuisance to utter them. "If it's . . . something worth, of course," he said at an even softer pitch, as if in soliloquy. The King wondered if there was something or someone in his thoughts. "He is invisible. His means . . . invisible. It renders a purer fiction."

"Rather like God," the King said, not taking his eyes off his book.

"A most difficult illusion to create."

Francis Bacon could make the King anxious the same way Shakespeare did. He also knew there was more to this invitation than dialogue on an ancient text. And the King was not up to his usual smut. Francis found him sober, almost solemn. "We are told you spend much time in the company of the man Shakespeare."

"He is a friend, Majestie. I prize his fellowship." His pitch rose.

"Indeed?"

"His gifts, as the age itself will attest, are prodigious. In his carriage he may be understated, but beneath that unremarkable visage is true genius, first among its kind, without peer or precedent." Francis understood the King's fondness for alliteration. He spoke with his usual certitude, if not a touch of audacity, considering his audience. "Time will prove generous to his name, Majestie. England will boast of him mightily in ages to come."

Francis felt the nakedness one feels when having said too much. Still, he had validated the King's suspicions concerning the Poet. Francis employed more daring than caution in his choice of words, wary, as he was, of the King's usual pounce. But his words did no conspicuous harm. The King had some business in his thought, and instead of the usual preamble or sermon, he came right to the point.

"We desire private audience with him at Richmond at the end of the month, and wish you to mediate, to acquire him for us, to be our ambassador." The King understood Bacon's fondness for the repetitive, as he called the device himself.

"Of course, Majestie, but I would think my Lord of South-ampton the better embassage, being his former patron." Francis knew Wriothesley to be an unworthy candidate. It was a mild provocation to pry into the King's intent.

"The Earl lacks . . ." The King's mind was suddenly aflood with options, an entire lexicon at his disposal to satisfy a sudden sour taste in his mouth. Considering his audience, he settled on one with less drama. ". . . discretion." With the exception of Robert Cecil, Francis Bacon understood the King as well as any-one in the kingdom. He understood the economy of his words, the things he said without saying them, the commands made without making them. Three things were made clear to him. That Wriothesley suffers some displeasure of the King, that he is to share this intelligence with no one, and that if any enterprise with the Poet turns bad or goes sour, if damage is done, Bacon himself will be accountable. "We must remember his blood, Francis. Besides, there is some offense between them, some op-probrium that divides your poet and the Earl. No, Francis, it must be a man of station, yes, but someone he is comfortable with. A friend." Anticipating the lawyer's next question, the King continued. "Do not ask us why, or for what reason we seek him now. In good time, Francis. In good time. Our desire of him is a private one, and a benevolent. It will not diminish your standing with him. We assure you, it is a small service for your king."

Bacon said nothing else. The King's command would not be questioned further. When Bacon left the privy chamber and stepped into the corridor, Robert Cecil was waiting for him nearby.

"Shall we walk together?" Bacon asked.

"What business with His Majestie?" Cecil asked with as much reserve as he was capable.

"Cousin, this is not like you. At least draw me into some craft, if but for sport."

The Cecils were never that charitable toward the Bacon brothers. Francis and Robert were always engaged, it seems, in some form of cobra and mongoose, their favorite pastime, shifting into some delicacy of speech only when it served them both. If the Cecils had a scrap of advantage they would hoard it, cultivate, and exploit it with a diabolical grace, meet for their own shrewd ends. They were always devising hurdles, some obstruction for their wiser, more capable cousins, particularly Francis, of whom Robert was secretly fretful. With smiles and tokens of amity, of course.

"I have no time for sport, Francis." The two men walked together, at the slower man's pace. "The King broods under the weight of some conceit, some stratagem, but says little. He is under the power of some charm of late. He mentions your poet often." Thinking of his friend, Francis could not disguise his amusement.

"Some commission I would guess," Bacon said. Cecil knew more than he confessed. Francis was certain of it. "Touching the translation perhaps?"

"Why do you laugh?" Cecil asked.

"Irony," the Philosopher said. "A grand one. The pulpits bark rabidly against the playhouses, while larding their sermons with the more memorable lines and gestures. They disguise the theft poorly, then blame the theatres for the plague, for God's sake."

"The King is reticent," Cecil interrupted. "When I inquired, he made no response, but spoke distractedly about the queen's annoying headaches." True to the sport between them, Cecil receded, obligating Francis to an opinion.

"Will is a dramatist, neither political nor theological." He tried to imagine the Poet in the company of men like Lancelot Andrewes and Ned Lively.

"This interview with the King has little to do with matters of state."

Francis laughed. In spite of Cecil's evolved instincts of statecraft, Francis was the master in these contests, as nature favors the mongoose.

"The King *is* the state," Bacon replied. "If he coughs, if he soils his doublet with drink or gravy it is a matter of state." Cecil's countenance almost thawed into a grin.

"The companies are close to making an end."

"So I hear. Savile consults with me on occasion, as does Chaderton."

"Did they tell you the last step, the final assessment before the finished manuscript goes to Mr. Barker is the King himself? That he has leave to make what alterations he likes, that he indeed proposes to do so, that only Andrewes, Lively, and Barlow hold any power of annulment over him at all, which is not likely?"

"Not that the King would exercise the option."

"Perhaps not. But tell me this, Francis. If you have in your service the chief of our poets, and it is your name that is to brazen the most important political book in the realm, the one relic history itself will remember you by . . . well . . ."

"You say it most decisively, cousin," said the mongoose.

"Say nothing to Will. If our suspicions are correct, the King's intention is a private one. Do as he asks. Just bring him. The King must read surprise on the Poet's face. He has made you a part of this now, Francis, with compensations far beyond that of mediator. You know that. He knows your frustrations with the old queen."

Under Elizabeth, Francis Bacon fell out of favor even as he had begun to move upward. Cecil was the grit in the wheel. So far, with James, Francis has been denied the Attorney Generalship. For all his wit and maneuvering he had only achieved the rank of King's Counsel Extraordinary, a name that sounded large, but paid little in the way of money or stature.

"He is not inclined to admit it, but other than his own, of course, he considers your mind the most far seeing, most advanced mind in the kingdom," Cecil continued, speaking his native cobra. "He will make good use of it. He wants things to be kept quiet for now. That is why he wants you, Francis, and not Southampton to fetch the Poet. He has other uses for the Earl."

"It's just as well. I'm not sure Will would respond to Southampton with much more than distraction or mild contempt at the moment. We speak candidly, but on the rift between himself and the earl he is mute, a thing he does well. What do your informants tell you?"

"It may be over a woman. Or not. In faith, I do not know."

"Hoy-day, a conundrum."

"I regret I must leave you for now."

And the cobra slithered, or rather dragged himself sullenly away.

The palace at Richmond was the King's least favorite possession. For a private audience, therefore, far from all the usual suitors, meddlers, petitioners, and general business of court, it was ideal. Francis Bacon did as he was asked and delivered his friend to the palace. Once formalities were extended, the Philosopher left the two men alone.

"It is good to see you again, Master Shakespeare."

"Majestie."

The king studied the presence before him. The small flourish the Poet made had as much comedy in it as it did reverence—the stretch of his doublet, the droop and wrinkle of his hose. The King hid his amusement. He too had become plump as the English king. But the dramatist was in his world now. The props were real. And no matter how many times one stood in the presence of Majestie, if you were not a member of the royal household, a courtier, on the Privy Staff, or some other officer of the state, if you did not live continually amid all the gilt and polish, if your eyes had not yet grown dull to all the glittering images, you could easily be overcome by it.

The Poet could hardly disguise his awe. He had performed at court before, but this was different. He was in a king's chamber, seeing his own portly features reflected in the gold and silver that seemed to overlay everything.

"It is magnificent, isn't it?" He let the question suspend between them. The King's voice was warm, disarming, as the Poet had remembered it. He let his imagination feast. He could not help himself. It was a stage. He knew that. There was no want for drama. Like any stage, many scripts were played out, comedies and tragedies alike, the one difference being consequence. The plots and the intrigues were real. The blood spilled was not pig's blood. The blades were, like treachery itself, razor sharp. There were few repeat performances.

The King was right. It was magnificent.

The Poet was amused at his own admiration, childlike as it was. The King looked at the surroundings himself with an indifference all kings must feel.

"We confess your Scottish play unnerved us."[12]

"That was not our . . . my intention, Majestie. I was heartsick at causing you displeasure."

"You have to understand, Master Shakespeare, we have had direct dealing with these hags." The use of the majestic plural fascinated the Poet, unaccustomed as he was to its use beyond the stage. "When her Majestie was first come to us from Denmark, and her ship set sail, the winds were roused violently against her and by these same foul devils. You have the advantage of a stage, and the safety of your fancy. Your villains are but paintings. Ours are real. We had Mr. Tylney close you down because we felt we had no choice. We had to make a statement. If you were any less the craftsman you are, we would not have felt it so deeply."

The Poet said nothing. The King's Men had been shown such favor and benefaction by the Crown he never expected the voice of chastisement, though there was flattery in the complaint.

"There is a vitality about your work . . . a living quality that sets you apart, so unlike the works of other playmakers. When you give our court witches, with their rounds and their potions, you give them witches indeed. We thrilled at it, amazedly. We have never been so shaken by a play. That is why we took the action we took." The Poet, in spite of his restraint, could not help but smile inwardly at the King's summation. The King smiled back. Understanding between them was immediate.

"Majestie," the Poet said in the affirmative.

"It was your MERCHANT that first got our attention. Your Portia played the sorceress with me." The King wasn't saying the half of it. On the first court performance, in Act Four, the young man playing a young woman playing a young man directed his soliloquy to the King, often catching the King's eye (as the Poet instructed). "'Tis mightiest in the mightiest: it becomes, the thronèd monarch better than his crown,'" the King said. "Indeed," he added. He quoted the entire passage.

"Majestie. Your possession . . ."

"But it is rather the work of a god, is it not?"

"I . . .?"

"You fashion worlds. You create order from chaos, determine who lives, who dies, who falls in love, who grieves, who laughs, all by your leave, by a toss of fancy. You give and take what life you choose. Time is your beadle. The sun rises or sets at the turn of a phrase, and with the color and spectacle you give it. In russet mantle clad. The earth spins another revolution at your slightest bidding. Mercy and judgment are in your power. Like God, your creation follows a script. It submits without question to your will . . . Will." The King laughed at his own joke. The Poet laughed with the King. It was an old joke, but merriment on the face of a monarch is a powerful thing.

"If your comparison holds, Majestie, and it does most royally, even the best of playmakers are but mimics, and poor ones at that. After two hours it has all been as incorporeal as a dream, a puff of smoke."

"Now you are being modest, William. Francis Bacon is convinced that history will speak your name with a pride reserved for those who have left the most indelible marks upon it—the conqueror, the pioneer . . . the monarch. We think you just might wear each of them well." The King had the rare ability to take speech from the Poet. "Your words move people, and that *is* power. There is nothing imaginary about that, nothing contrived. To have access to those places where men hide their hearts, ay, there it is, is it not? To rouse the sleeping and the dead, to enkindle the weak to brave acts, to alter kingdoms, to bring down the Philistine with the smooth polished stone of your wit."

The Poet was unaware he had aroused such ardor in the King.

"You do this with our common tongue, and most uncommonly," the King continued. "You put speech in the mouth of the tavern moll that is the envy of the gentlest courtier. But enough of that. Let's to the matter." In the hesitation that followed, anticipation mingled with promise of reward. "We will explain your commission forthwith, but first we must insist upon something." The King paused for acknowledgement.

"Majestie," the Poet assured.

"This is a private undertaking. Whatever burden we set upon thy shoulders, whatever rewards or honors we bestow upon thee, must be kept private. There will be no patent, no legal warrant or security, and no witnesses but ourself, Sir Francis, and the Lords Southampton and Salisbury, who are or will be sworn as well to this oath. And these men know not yet my darker purpose. Can you submit to these conditions?"

"What greater honor can one receive than the trust of their Sovereign?"

"Content?"

"Content, i' faith . . ." It slipped out of his mouth before he could call it back. The oath was not proper before a king. But it went unnoticed. The King was full of oaths himself. Being ignorant still of the commission of which the King continued to speak, the Poet's countenance did not fall, but suffered droop nonetheless. This did not escape the King's awareness but he chose to let the moment tarry, having royal possession of it. James had long thought about this encounter. The Poet idled in small agony over the commission he was still ignorant of.

Elizabeth had her *eyes*: Robert Dudley, the Earl of Leicester. She had her *oracle*: Sir Walter Raleigh. The small and ancient Archbishop Whitgift she called her *little black husband*. Robert Cecil was her *pygmy*. The former queen had an entire privy circus at her bidding. It was a *voice* James was after.

"You are aware, Master Shakespeare, are you not, that we have commissioned a new bible that will serve as a monument to our reign?"

"Yes, Majestie."

"You are to have a place in this work." The King paused, to let the notion settle. "We ask your patience, that we might explain the enterprise. Our country has suffered a religious divide for too long. I intend to heal this breach; to be the Solomon she inwardly longs for. This book is the physick that will heal the deep cleft in its heart and restore her former glories." The Poet was patient, his imagination warm. The King's eyes brightened in recognition of both. His pace quickened.

"Unlike your Lear, we intend to bring together the severed branches of our kingdom. Richard Bancroft, Lancelot Andrewes, and ourself created the architecture for the translation and the rule that governs it. The participants were handpicked, according to their particular gifting. There is no need to burden you with the whole method. The translator's task is not to innovate, that is, not to create novelty, or even a new translation, but to choose the best existing lines, the richest and truest text from previous English translations and weave them together using what invention necessary to arrive at the finest rendering of the scripture, and by a single governing aesthetic. The language is to be set forth gorgeously. That is our principal command."

The Poet was unsure what was being asked of him, but the King was making a superb argument for it.

"Once the drafts of each company are sifted and refined," the King continued, "it is up to the directors of the companies to compile them into one manuscript, one single draft. The same pattern of sifting and refining is followed once again, only by twelve men instead of the six companies. It is now 1608, almost 1609. The work is nearing completion and will be in our possession, we are told, by month's end. As a craftsman you can understand the rigor, the pains that have been taken." The Poet made no response. The King receded into a kind of imperial gravity.

"There is but one more step the translation is to take." He stared at the Poet with his odd tortured gaze, his mind alive with enterprise. "Before we go into that, there is one condition we have insisted upon throughout. Accuracy, yes, as much as is possible. But there is something else, something that to us is more precious." The King's eyes ablaze. "I have insisted that the voice reflect the reign, that it reflect our person. The language must be the best that is in us. And there is not a poet among them." The King's voice was pleasant, but punctuated with emphasis. "This is a work of an elevated spirit, charged with the dread and moment of Highness itself. Because it is breathed of God, divinity must sparkle on its pages. It demands a wordcraft beyond that of the prelate . . . or the academic."

The ellipsis suspended optimistically between the Poet and the King.

"We have watched you from some distance," the King continued. "We have recorded your best lines, as has half our kingdom. We know it is not prudent for a king to admit such, to speak so precipitously, so transparently, but this is bigger than ourself, bigger than crowns and scepters. Let us say it in a way you will understand. 'I have not art to reckon my groans.' And there it is, is it not?" The King halted. The Poet remained quiet. "The manuscript is currently being read by a small elite community of translators at Stationer's Hall for further refinement. I believe you know Sir John Bois. One step remains. That is, ourself. It comes at last to our eyes alone for a final sifting."

Understanding dramatic suspension, the Poet remained silent. It was a long pitch, and yet brief by his usual standards. Even the King knew better than to waste his passion in excess verbiage before a poet.

"Aye, and now we come to you, Master Shakespeare," the King said at last. "We have long thought of this time. For the past four years, since the notion first came to us, we have kept no one's counsel but our own. We kept ourself aloof from the enterprise, got in no one's way. We made lengthy estimation of the companies laboring over our book, and in doing so the decision became an easy one for us. They have given us something quite wonderful, and yet . . . the enterprise is not finished. For it is in desperate want of a poet." The King paused, and to his delight, the Poet said nothing. "We will explain, so that you may understand your commission."

"Majestie," the Poet replied quietly, a comma to the loquacious King.

"Majestie is not some lone glittering star, but a living force, a capable and terrible force. Our new translation must reflect this Majestie above all things—glorious, incandescent, gorgeous. We must give back to God the highest and the best that is in our language and in ourselves. Majestie—solemn, terrible, imposing Majestie. Lucid, resplendent, express, consecrated. Like the waters that cover the sea, so this great metal must gild our reign. Do you mark me, William?"

The King seemed almost outside himself in these moments, to the great admiration of the Poet. The contrast of what he had witnessed for himself in this private chamber and the report of others, all the claims of bombast and smutty jest, against the eloquence and providence by which the King now spoke was difficult to reconcile. He began to entertain an entirely new and promising vision of the piteous king, who, at that moment, was not in character but in himself. This was not dramaturgy. It was belief. The Poet said little, if anything, choosing to nurse the charm, to feed quietly upon it, as to have it pass.

"Majestie" the Poet said again, in the affirmative.

"Good." The King's smile was the sun at daybreak. "Good," he said again. "This is why you alone will pilot this work to its completion. We have detected in you a refinement, a trim, an understatement I do not detect in others. The weight of true Majestie would o'erwhelm lesser poets. They would fall to flattery, hyperbole, or self-interest. I trust your economies."

The King gave little time for the thought to saturate, but continued with the business at hand. "We can't impress upon you enough our single condition. No one is to know of your involvement in this. No one. You are to work in an assigned chamber here, at Richmond. The theaters will close. Plague is a

common threat, so detection will be less likely. Do you understand what we ask of thee?"

"Majestie." The word nodded favorably.

"Will you swear an oath of secrecy to your king?"

"Yes."

"You will be paid a thousand pound for your service. Does that
content?" The number made an impression. The King could see it.
"Cecil will make the arrangements." The Poet thought little of the
anonymity. He welcomed it. The sound of dropping coin was the
sweeter music. Glory could not feed you, put a roof over your head,
or please the wife back home. He might still hope for a knighthood.

"Due to the vexations of state that will beg our attention,
Lord Robert will intercede where I cannot. He will not interfere
with your work but will see to it that you have what materials
you require. You need but ask. Is this meet?"

"Yes, Majestie."

"Now, to the work itself. The Crown in this one regard will
be in your power. Perhaps you will need to change very little.
That lies in your discretion, your power alone. Each alteration
you make though, however slight, I wish you to document. Here
is a copy of the manuscript, the translator's final draft. When you
make an alteration, mark it here with our initials, IR."[13] The king
pointed to the left (verso) side of the open draft. "Where the voice
is . . . wooden, where it wrangles, the pitch bent or otherwise
abused, where it lumbers or plods sluggishly about, apply your
art. I assume your compensation is agreeable?"

"Yes, Majestie."

As the King continued, the Poet began to consider what
kind of Polonius he might have made, Malvolio, or Lear—quietly, to himself, of course.

"You have friends here. Sir Francis, and our lords of Pembroke and Southampton. Our departed cousin, Essex, spoke well of you in his letters to us. Do this for your king, and you will have made a friend above all friends."

"I am bereft of words."

"Then we will take back our fee." The King laughed his thick laugh.

"Perhaps not *all* of them, Majestie."

"Spare, subtle modification," the King stressed. "Touches."

The Poet smiled. All the particulars of their interview weighed and considered, it was the high moment of his life, or one of them. He also felt a great sympathy for the King, and in a way he could not explain. Part visionary, part fool, part tyrant, part medicine man, part monarch, part jester, the Poet felt at ease in the royal presence. He felt nothing like that with the old queen, yet he knew her to be the stronger of the two monarchs. Majestie was more than a mere preoccupation with this king; it was a matter of faith itself, of belief both old and deep. He had been branded with it from birth. It was all he knew.

Long before Francis Bacon made it a proverb, James knew that knowledge is power, that the powerful need to have all the knowledge available to them. It was one of the few useful habits he had acquired over the years. Forced to gorge, digest, and metabolize outrageous amounts of information under his old tutor, George Buchanan, the young king developed a mind to receive, to organize, and to catalogue. James was good at this.

Since the notion first came to him to use the Poet as his literary First Minister, the King took it upon himself to learn all he could about the man. The more he learned, however, the less he was impressed. It had to be some trick of a paradoxical scheming god, he reasoned, the whole *first shall be last* business or *the least shall be greatest*. He decided it best to give Providence the benefit of the doubt.

He considered the lack of education, or at least the quality of education the Poet had with no small amazement. Sartorially tidy, rich but not gaudy or overstated, he considered what little weight the man seemed to carry about him, the sheer lack of presence. Congenial, affable, agreeable, he seemed to possess none of the fire, strangeness, or high spirit of Marlowe or the bully Jonson. The King had never met Marlowe, nor wanted to, but the endless stories fascinated and terrified him at the same time—the brooding poet, the untamed man of words, the seductive melancholia, the man of shadows. Shakespeare had none of Marlowe's eccentricities. He seemed as plain and understated as his work seemed copious and grand. English sterling was his muse. He seemed more the well-dressed shopkeeper than a colossus.

"Jesu," the King chortled, "he is like the old queen."

The King's Men thought better of HAMLET that afternoon at Hampton Court. The principals considered it too long for the King. They witnessed in horror as James slept through one play already and walked out of another. One of the unfortunates was written by a friend of the Bacon brothers, Robert Burton, and the other by Ben Jonson. Not wanting to suffer a similar fate, the King's Men performed THE MERCHANT OF VENICE instead, to the delight of the King.

CHAPTER FIVE

Your Sweetest Sense

THE SKY WAS OVERCAST, but it did not rain until late afternoon. The King was waiting in the Henry VII Chamber when he arrived. After being announced, and making a show of courtesy, the Poet approached the table where the King was looking over the translation, some meditation idling in the royal mind. He studied the oddly tilted creature—the exaggerated codpiece, the comic shuffle of his feet, the wariness of his leg, his tragic vanity. "Where it is dull," the King said still looking at the draft, "where the gleam of Majestie is absent or mute, where the music lacks form or splendor, tune the pegs so to speak. Do you understand?"

"I am moved at your Majestie's confidence." It was out of his mouth before he could stop it.

"Do only what the line asks of you. Nothing more. Only,

and let us be clear, enhance the music that is present already. Do you mark me?"

"I assure your Majestie I do." The Poet had reserves of patience for his sovereign.

"A touch, Master Shakespeare, a touch. It is one voice we desire, from first to last." the King added. "Do your best to disappear, if you understand our meaning." The Poet made a small gesture of approval. "Observe notes in the margin if there be any. Respect them if you can, but apply your cunning, your sweetest sense, if but for the sake of one word only."

"Truth needs no color with his color fix'd," the Poet said distractedly, "Beauty no pencil . . ."[14]

"What's that?"

"I understand you well, Majestie."

"But enough of that. Let us look at an example together."

"I have something in mind, if I may. But my memory lags."

"What do you remember of it?"

"Something touching a man's gift, bringing him . . ."

"Bringing him before princes?" With a lift in his voice.

"Majestie."

The King opened the manuscript before them, a quarto bound with three leather threads at the spine, scripture on the right (recto) side, the left (verso) reserved for notes. Sifted by so many eyes and ears—examining, prodding, adding, subtracting, adding again, deflowering, inspecting, throwing out, throwing back in, throwing out again, debating, fighting, chewing, spitting, gnashing teeth—it was a clean volume. There were surprisingly few notes, and these were only of the more questionable renderings.

James knew his scripture. Thanks to his inflexible childhood tyrant-tutor Buchanan, James read Greek and Latin before he was five. But the young king never developed much of a taste for Hebrew. The "glottal hack," as he liked to call it, was too much to ask of his speech apparatus. "A tongue" he said, "rendered from drinking too much goat's milk," he told the Poet, his words smelling of alcohol. He never liked Jews anyway.

The King had a theory about Arabic as well, though, like his Hebrew, he knew no word of it. If the Turk himself unnerved the oft-berattled King, and he did, the rhythms of the language fascinated him, if in a private way—its musical canter, its down-up-up-down-up | down-up-up-down-up cadence. How it seems "to gargle its words," he said. "They are a nomadic people. The rhythms of their tongue developed on the back of camels while carrying on simple conversation, side by side, generation after generation. The animal is due some credit." When the King demonstrated the theory, holding imaginary reins, moving at a slow uneven trot about the room, speaking his gibberish Arabic, the royal guard rushed in. When they saw the figure of the King leaning against the Poet, and the two of them laughing convulsively with one another, the alarm deflated. The King nodded to the guard and gave them leave to return to their post.

Regaining composure, he turned again to the Poet.

His eyes moving over the text, James mumbled something in his own strain of English. He then read aloud. "Proverbs. 'A man's gift enlargeth his way and bringeth him before great men.'" The words throttled midsentence and became mercilessly bound together in the royal mouth with little hope of rescue. The Poet remained expressionless. Grateful to his sense of dramatic timing, in the exact fraction of it he spoke, and with a measured grace.

"May I?"

The King moved out of the way.

The Poet looked at the text for some time, said nothing, made no facial expressions. The silence was not cumbersome, even to the King whose energies would hardly ever allow him to remain still. "Perturbation of the blood," said one of his surgeons. "Conflict of humours," said another. The small poetry covered their lack of understanding of their trade. "Damned giddy Scot," Jonson said.

According to the notes made by one of His Majestie's translators, LC, perhaps Laurence Chaderton, the Hebrew word is גדול [*gadowl*], which means "the great." The verb, "*enlargeth*," stalled and recoiled in the King's mouth. The line needed to be less work. Referring to the Bishop's Bible, he read, "A mans gyft maketh an open way." According to the notes, רחב [*rachab*], means "to be or grow wide." He began to whisper the fragment to himself. How it all metabolized he could not explain, to the King or to himself. He just knew it when he heard it. There were also limitations he was obliged to acknowledge. The translators did the tedious job of checking their work against ancient manuscripts, so there was small room to work. To anyone else this might have been a handicap.

Had James asked him in those moments what he might be thinking, he is not sure he would have been able to answer.

It was not time for thinking. Thinking was wide of the point.

Crossing out the offending phrase, he wrote his final thoughts above the line. The King examined the alteration, quietly, without expression. It was a cruder hand than he was accustomed, but in spite of its lack of polish, it was legible. He read the line.

A man's gift ~~enlargeth his way~~ maketh room for him
and bringeth him before great men.

It was a small change, but it did not toil in the King's mouth.
The King approved the text, the first of countless approvals.

The King suspected the Poet was playing a game of sorts,
considering the scripture he chose. Even so, he said nothing.
James read it as a tribute from the Poet, a tipping of his hat. It
was a thousand pound well spent.

The King dismissed himself and left the Poet to his work.

Belonging once to Henry VII, the table before him was mas-
sive, thick as a ship's hull—legs, bulbous and masterfully carved,
some sea creature coiled at its feet. At his disposal as he might
have need of them and arranged side by side were the many
Bible translations used by the translators—folios, quartos, and
other odd old ends.

The folios were cumbersome, though decorative, some with
brass latches, all with the look of money, ostentation, and gravity. In the center of the table, closest to him, was the translator's draft. It was divided into parts by companies, he assumed,
though loosely bound as a single unit.

It wasn't the first time he had been commissioned by royalty,
but this time the pay was better, and the company. Elizabeth,
upon seeing his Falstaff, fell hard for the paunch knight. He appealed to the bawd in her, matching her in wit, age, vanity, even
belly. Old and worn by the turn of the century, no amount of
paint could call back her former glory. All but toothless and of

difficult temper, her once renowned humor had by long decline given way to bombast and mild paranoia. Requesting another play featuring the round man, the Poet gave her Majestie THE MERRY WIVES OF WINDSOR. A middling piece of work, written more from obedience than inspiration, Sir John was present in name, though not in belly.

"It took nearly a fortnight to write the bloody thing," he told Francis.

On her death, Shakespeare was asked to write the queen's eulogy, an honor of great weight. Fearing no reprisal from the future king, he turned down the offer. The old queen may have liked his Falstaff, but she did not prize his Hamlet. All of the Poet's questions about her were answered in the choice. Not that he loved Falstaff less, but he loved Hamlet more. Truth is, she saw her Essex in the Dane and turned him away.

The Poet looked upon this present commission with a different hope.

He decided it best to ease into the task, to graze, and at the speed of one of his longer poems perhaps. The fire cracked. He stared distractedly at the furnishings, which only prolonged his reverie—the plush couches, the tapestries, the damask, the dark woods, the skin of gold that seemed to laminate everything, including his commission, the portraits on the wall, one of Henry VII, the other Elizabeth of York, or so he assumed, the quality of the writing instruments, the royal supply.

He could not help but feel the good fortune of his appointment, that the King would have such appetite for his talent. He had charmed the muse, and she repaid his kindness by enlarging both his name and his purse.

He was idling.

Without provocation or reason, and with a slight shudder of nerve he thought of his cousin, the Jesuit, Robert Southwell, who he hadn't thought of in many years. He shook himself free of it, and turned his gaze toward the work.

One by one, he began examining the volumes on the table. Closest to the translator's draft was the Bishop's Bible, stodgy and imperious. He could hardly lift it. A copy of the Latin Vulgate, the Matthews Bible, and a well-preserved edition of the Wycliffe Bible were also within reach. He didn't bother examining all the volumes. His commission would demand close examination soon enough.

The King hated the Geneva Bible above all English bibles. It had something to do with the excessive use of the word *tyrant* where other translations most often used the word *king*. It was the one bible the Poet was familiar with. There was no copy of the Geneva Bible anywhere on the royal premises.

At the outermost edge of the table, looking as if it had been placed there more by oversight than intention, was a small, worn, and poorly bound bible, in octavo.[15] But the squat little book moved him in ways the others did not. He thought of his Bassanio. Unlike the other books on the table, there was no clear title on the cover. There were marks and small furrows that resembled the shape of letters perhaps or some cover design, but they were so worn with age and use it was difficult to make them out. And it didn't appear to have an author. The date on the cover page was 1526. Other than the Wycliffe version of 1395, the octavo was the oldest English translation on the table. He scanned a few of his favorite passages and read the words softly to himself. The words were familiar in his mouth.

The spirite is willynge but the flesshe is weake.

He read the same passage in the translator's final draft. It was identical. "You did well to leave it alone," he said to himself. To make any alteration, however slight, or to read the passage any other way would dull its music and extinguish the flame of memory. He continued in this manner, comparing one text against another, reading the small volume (the octavo) first.

For in him we lyve move and have oure beynge as certayne of youre awne Poetes sayde.

Again, he turned to the same passage in the translator's draft. As he had hoped, other than the spelling, the line was once again identical. He breathed a sigh of relief. In this remote, though royal chamber, and under a commission no history would record, he had discovered a major English voice, an original, a poet-scholar from his grandfather's time, whoever it was, the knowledge of which delighted him, shocked and petrified him in one swift twist of passion. There was evidence of this old voice everywhere. His own English was infected with it.

The work suddenly seemed manageable, now that he was fully introduced.

The Poet was acquainted with many of the King's translators. Ben Jonson introduced him to Henry Savile years earlier at the new Bodleian Library at Oxford. Savile's association with Jonson was usually over some matter of Greek, but Savile loved nothing more than the English word. He was crazy about language. And books. Lady Margaret, Savile's wife, once said, "I would I were a book," hoping her Henry would pay better attention to her. "Then it would be better that you be an almanac," her Henry said in response, "then I could change you every year."

Savile took a real interest in Shakespeare, which only aggravated Jonson. They met often at the Crown Tavern in Oxford. It was Savile who introduced the Poet to the brilliant though absentminded John Bois, also at the Crown, an establishment managed by George and the lovely Jennet Davenant.

Many of the translators, whether they admitted it publicly or not, had appetite for the theater. It couldn't be helped. It was a theatrical culture. Like the Poet, most of them were older, seasoned men, men of stature, some, like Savile, of great belly, and Elizabethans all (though no such word existed at the time). They had all been weaned on the Elizabethan sonnet, the Poet's own among them, a sound he helped cultivate.

Though he had a better idea of the task before him, he was not yet ready to make a formal start. He held the octavo in his hand most of the time. He opened it and read from the First Epistle of John.

That which was from the begynninge concerninge which we have hearde which we have sene with oure eyes which we have loked vpon and oure hondes have hadled of the worde of life.

Something stumbled in his mouth as he read the lines. He found and read the same passage in the translator's draft. The passages were identical. He read it again, still bothered by some stitch, some annoyance he could not define. He thought of the King and considered what the phrase might do in the royal mouth. He was certain it would toil there, and with more violence than was fair to ask of anyone.

He walked over to the window and looked out at the Thames. His thoughts slowed to the speed of the small crafts drifting by. Still tightly wound considering his new work environment, after a bit of daydreaming he returned to the table and crossed out a single word.

The action felt strange. Some fifty or more clerics and scholars, handpicked by His Majestie, had spent nearly five years sifting through old documents to give the English scripture a more refined music, to give the reign new polish, and here he is judge and captain over their effort. But it is His Majestie's Bible. It is His Majestie's coin and seal behind the great work. And a commission from the King is a commission from the King. The Poet is required to judge and to act upon his judgment independent of all other considerations. He read the line again, with the edit.

> That which was from ye beginning ~~concerninge,~~ which wee haue heard, which wee haue seen with our eyes, which wee haue looked upon, and our hands haue handled of the word of life.

The deletion of a single word made all the difference to his ear. The passage did not fight back but stepped gracefully where it bridled only moments before. Those were his thoughts anyway. Beyond that, he had no explanation, nor did he think one necessary. It sounded better. That is all.

He made the King's mark, the IR, as instructed.

It was his second act as the King's ghostwriter, and though he had done very little, he had made a formal start.

Once again, he thought of his dead cousin, and once again for no conspicuous reason. All his present goodwill soured with his risen ghost. He winced inwardly as the entire history uploaded into his thoughts.

Before being captured by agents of the queen in 1595, Robert Southwell published a collection of poems called ST. PETER'S COMPLAINT. The preface was dedicated "To my worthy good cosen, Maister W. S." It was the obligation of poets, Southwell wrote, to offer their gifts in service to God. Staring at a table full of bibles, the Poet spoke the words aloud, the memory intact, uncorrupted.

> Poets, by abusing their talents, and making the follies and feignings of love the customary subject of their base endeavours, have so discredited this faculty, that a poet, a lover, and a liar, are by many reckoned but three words of one signification. But the vanity of men cannot counterpoise the authority of God, who delivered many parts of Scripture in verse, and, by His Apostle willing us to exercise our devotion in hymns and spiritual sonnets, warranteth the art to be good, and the use allowable . . .

His tongue felt dry. When the Poet first received his copy of ST. PETER'S COMPLAINT, in spite of its plea, his response was not unexpected. His Jesuit cousin simply asked too much of him. To dedicate his art to God alone was not what he came to London for. He could not afford to put on a collar, even if he wanted to. He had a wife and three kids back in Stratford, and the "worthy good" cousin's star was on the rise. With the popularity of his HENRY VI plays years earlier, then the RICHARDS II and III, he wasn't about to stop, or slow down.

Typical of London street creatures, his first response was to bridle. Southwell's plea had such power in him at the time he had little choice but to strike back where he knew Southwell would be listening. The Poet received a copy of the COMPLAINT not long after ROMEO AND JULIET opened at The Curtain. In a new play he was writing at the time, he hardly bothered to disguise his theft of Southwell's "a poet, a lover, and a lyar . . ."

> The lunatic, the lover and the poet
> Are of imagination all compact:
> One sees more devils than vast hell can hold,
> That is, the madman: the lover, all as frantic,
> Sees Helen's beauty in a brow of Egypt:
> The poet's eye, in fine frenzy rolling,
> Doth glance from heaven to earth, from earth to heaven;
> And as imagination bodies forth
> The forms of things unknown, the poet's pen
> Turns them to shapes and gives to airy nothing
> A local habitation and a name.[16]

In the same play, he put scripture (or something like scripture) in the mouth of a humble creature, Nick Bottom the Weaver.

The eye of man hath not heard,
the ear of man hath not seen,
man's hand is not able to taste, his tongue to conceive,
nor his heart to report, what my dream was.

With a slight blush he opened the octavo, still in his hand, found and read the scripture Bottom so mercilessly befouled.

The eye hath not sene and the eare hath not hearde nether have entred into the herte of man ye thinges which God hath prepared for them that love him.

He read the same passage in the translator's draft.

Eye hath not seene, nor eare heard, neither haue entred into the heart of man, the things which God hath prepared for them that loue him.

He preferred the octavo, the old text to its heir, but left it alone, and made no changes in the line. He felt a slight tremor of conscience, albeit a small one, that he had abused the old text with such alacrity.

It wasn't easy to dismiss his cousin's ghost. He was no longer holding the octavo in his hand and couldn't remember setting it back on the table. Regaining himself, as he felt it prudent to do, he stopped all movement and stood quietly for a moment. In that instant, he began to hear music playing somewhere. It was pleasant but faint, with an aerial quality, as if being performed in some remove of the palace. He thought little of it and continued his work.

He was finding his way, making only small modifications, experimenting, navigating around his commission. He understood the wisdom of inspired idling and was good at it. He understood that order and art, like love and reason, by their very natures, must be, at times, indifferent one to the other. It had never been his practice, for instance, to start with one, and proceed to two, then three, and so on. He had his linear side, certainly, but he just as often wrote the end of a play before ever considering how it might begin. The passages that attracted him at first needed few changes, if any, be it some fault in construction or a matter of pitch, but he knew language too well to think the work would always progress smoothly, without obstruction.

One of his favorite bible characters was Elijah, the cantankerous Old Testament prophet. Though out of fashion for some time, he had always considered writing a play about Elijah and Jezebel (a consideration that made the Office of the Revels shudder). Elijah didn't have the poetry of a Job, a Jeremiah, or a David, but he was great theater, and he was magnificently flawed. The prophet had the dimensions of Lear or Antony. Ruined souls always entertain. He riffled through the translator's draft until he found what he was after in 1 Kings. He spoke the words to himself, drifting, as was his custom, into a kind of meditation.

> . . . and beholde, the LORD passed by, and a great and strong winde rent the mountaines, and brake into pieces the rockes, before the LORD; but the LORD was not in the wind: and after the wind an earthquake, but the LORD was not in the earthquake. And after the earthquake a fire, but the LORD was not in the fire: and after the fire, a small still voice.

There were a few notes scattered about the margin, none of which were any consequence to him, many in Latin, jots and scribbles he could hardly make out, and a host of initials, among them LA, whom he assumed was Lancelot Andrewes, the largest spirit among the translators. He met Andrewes at a performance of HAMLET at Hampton Court the first summer of the new reign. Andrewes had a reputation of being the best preacher of the age. James was known to sleep with his sermons under his pillow. The Bishop of Carlisle in RICHARD II was fashioned after Andrewes, or Andrewes was flattered by the assumption that he was. Like the King, Andrewes was privately awed at the virtuosity of the Poet, in spite of his lack of presence. As much as he tried not to speak the lines in his private chambers, the chief translator could not resist. "Fear not, my lord. That Power that made you king hath power to keep you king in spite of all."[17]

Of course, to be fair, the Poet had heard Lancelot Andrewes preach on many occasions, noting each dramatic movement, each rise and fall of passion, each gradation of thought, however delicate, making use of all he observed. He always thought Andrewes would have made a great Claudius, Brutus, or a particularly fine Henry IV.

The Poet repeated the lines, at times only moving his lips. It was a phantom he sought, something elusive that came with years of deep listening. He would know it when he heard it.

". . . *but the LORD was not in the fire: and after the fire, a small still voyce.*"

He wasn't sure why it bothered him, but it did.

After meditating on the line with no results, and to distract himself he took note of his surroundings. One of the more modest rooms in the palace, it was nonetheless decked with the

finest appointments in the realm, imported from all over the
known world. His own workspace was Spartan, having more the
charm of a cellar or a humble garret than the palace of a king.
He turned to the Wycliffe Bible. With patience, he found and
read the passage.

> And aftir the stiryng is fier; not in the fier is the Lord.
> And aftir the fier is the issyng of thinne wynd; there
> is the Lord.

He reached for one of the other bibles, by Coverdale, and
read the passage.

> And after the earth quake there came a fyre, but the
> LORDE was not in the fyre. And after the fyre came
> there a styll softe hyssinge.

He felt as if it were dragging its feet. It was a kind of certainty he was looking for, an internal agreement he would be
able to hear, that most often settled somewhere in his belly. But
he would have no satisfaction for the moment, and he would not
fight it. He made a mental note, turned back to the octavo, and
searched elsewhere.

> For Christ is to me lyfe and deeth is to me a vauntage.

"'ow now . . . whose mare just died," he muttered, his *h*
silent.

The Burbage in his head might have been able to ransom
such a text, as he was often called on to do, but there was no

fire in the line, nothing to warm his heart. The *Bishop's Bible*, which he was already weary of, read with the same flat note, like marble or alabaster. It plagiarized Tyndale, note for note, as did the translator's draft, and without improvement.

He scratched his head figuratively and continued.

It wasn't until he came to the Wycliffe translation that he began to sense the low sweet hum of recognition. "For me to lyue is Christ, and to die is wynnyng." It was an improvement, he thought, but it did not satisfy. His step was so bound to a ten-syllable line he sped through one synonym, one construction after another, exhausting every possible inflection, combination, and permutation, the dizzy math often required to render a sim-ple thread of text. He crossed out the line in the translator's draft and in its place wrote the following:

For to liue is Christ and to die is gaine.

He had an old love for the monosyllable—English, French, Anglo-Saxon, it didn't matter. He read the line again. While it appealed to his sense of rhythm, after reading a marginal note in the translator's draft made by John Bois concerning the prepo-sitional phrase "to me," (ζαω εμοι) he reconsidered the edit in favor of Bois, whose friendship (and wit) he treasured. Making the adjustment, the final and twice-altered text read:

For to me to liue is Christ, and to die is gaine.

It was his first formidable modification.

Until that moment it was about language, the charm of sound, the generosity of coin. Now, sharing a room full of old bibles and with the meddling ghost of his departed cousin, he suspects there may be more to his commission than first anticipated.

He tries not to think about that.

The line performs as it was asked to. As he makes the identifying mark, he feels a sense of pride unlike any he has felt before.

"Why, what a king this is!" says the Horatio in his head.

CHAPTER SIX

What a Piece of Work

IT WAS AGREED THAT THE KING ALONE would review his work. With the Poet standing nearby, the King read the altered passage in Philippians. "For to me to liue is Christ, and to die is gaine." His speech was sober, the performance effortless. He then compared the original passage as the translators set it down and shook his royal head with conspicuous delight. As he studied the document, moving at times about the great table, the King leaned on the Poet, who planted his feet firmly without fuss, as he had seen Cecil and others do. Though close proximity to the King had its own challenges, His Majestie read slowly, in a casual manner, shifting his weight often as needed, warming himself in a private revelation and self-inflicted lauds. It is the mark of true greatness, he thought to himself, to choose greatly.

Not one to underestimate the value of cerebral vacancy in the procession of art, the Poet started fanning pages of the draft, effecting a kind of self-hypnosis. He was even known to sing on occasion, quietly, to himself, of course. *When that I was and a tiny little boy* . . . His voice, like him, older, quieter, bent in places. . . . *with a hey ho, the wind and the rain.* He thought about the swarm of divines and scholars, men of name and pedigree who labored over the immense work, who knew nothing of his presence among them, nor ever would.

Then sigh not so, but let them go, and be you blithe and bonny . . . converting all your sounds of woe, into hey nonny, nonny.

His thoughts often sounded like that. Only rarely did they turn on him.

He wasn't at Tyburn the morning of his cousin's execution, in spite of the buzz and the crowd it generated. He had no taste for crude entertainments. TITUS ANDRONICUS was theater. It was gore and slapstick. Tyburn was real. And ROMEO AND JULIET was playing at The Curtain that same afternoon.

The news of Southwell's imprisonment and the primitive cruelties he suffered under the queen's rackmaster-rapist-torturer Sir Richard Topcliffe did not escape his attention. He thought Robert Southwell a gifted poet, with an elevated mind, a Hamlet in cleric's weeds. He also thought him a fool for wasting his gifts on spiritual matters, most particularly as lethal as they could prove to be in so formerly a Catholic England. None of this kept him from admiring Southwell's poetry. He devoured every poem, every fragment of prose the Jesuit ever wrote, and with appetite, printing much of it to memory. To say it didn't affect his work is perhaps not to look close enough.

He shook off the ghost.

It didn't take long for the Poet to become enamored with the waddling king. He could not have created so unlikely a character under any heaven of invention, however bright. A kind of tenderness developed between them, a mutual submission the Poet treasured in spite of the usual alehouse buzz about "Queen James" or the "tottering state," a crude reference to the trouble in the King's legs posed once by an innkeeper. He shook off the reverie and returned again to his task.

> Iesus Christe yesterday and to day, and the same foreuer.

Reading the Bishop's Bible, he told himself, was like watching the King eat. He opened the octavo hoping for improvement, but found none.

> Iesus Christ yesterdaye and to daye and the same continueth for ever.

The translator's final rendering of the text was identical to the Bishop's Bible. Mildly aggravated, judgment was swift. "The condition is the point, ma'am," he said to the image of Elizabeth of York on the wall, "the sameness." With a snip here and a stitch there, the translator's draft now read:

> Iesus Christ the same yesterday, and to day, and ~~the same~~ for euer.

He knew he might be taking liberties with the Greek, but he also knew the King would approve his modification. A wash of contentment came over him, the sweet and affirming YES. Out of curiosity he opened the Wycliffe Bible and read the same passage.

Jhesu Crist, yistirdai, and to dai, he is also unto the worldis.

Neither the Poet nor the translators depended too much on Wycliffe's text, white around its muzzle as it was. But it never disappointed.

Weary after a session, he stepped into the carriage for the long ride back to Silver Street and his lodging at the Mountjoy's. He had to give Cecil his due. Everything was arranged for him, at his convenience.

A dense fog settled over his thoughts, though the night itself, or most of it, was clear. The rain had abated. Clouds had given way and opened a large hole in the sky, the moon one big bright eye. The carriage was plain for one of the royal fleet. Cecil thought it prudent to draw as little attention as possible. It was still the finest carriage the Poet had yet ridden in. There was just enough mud and uneven road to make him drowsy, the increase in his belly shifting indelicately about.

He closed his eyes and let his imagination feed.

Against all the successes, the small but significant modifications he made on the translation so far, he could not shake the passage from 1 Kings. The carriage had hardly reached Chiswick before he had exhausted the passage, repeating fragments, and making no judgment. Aggravated, he lifted his head and looked out the window. Seeing the spires of Westminster, he called out to the driver.

"Sir, I would depart here." The carriage stopped. "The night is crisp," he said, "I will the rest of the way on foot." He offered the driver a gratuity. The driver ignored him, tapped the reins, and slowly pulled away.

The rain had stopped but the mud came up to the buckles on his shoes. He stepped as quickly as he could out of the thoroughfare onto some grass nearby. Once clear of the mud, he regretted having let the carriage and driver go. He massaged his hand. Days earlier while making an alteration to a passage in Job, of all books, he noticed a slight tremor he could not control. He thought nothing of it at the time, thinking it a result of overwork.

He had achieved what no other poet in the realm had achieved. Against smug prejudice, no play had been performed at either Cambridge or Oxford, being perceived, as it was, beneath university standards. HAMLET changed all that. HAMLET changed him. HAMLET was his making. He had money. He had a lot of money. He had stature as a poet. He had served two monarchies, a great queen and a great king. He bought New House in Stratford and was yet to enjoy it. "Five Gables" he sometimes called it.

He thought of his son on occasion, and his father.

For the next few days he continued in the same manner, gravitating to the most familiar passages, not realizing he had made a start. With the octavo in his hand, he read the following passage from the gospel of Matthew.

> Come unto me all ye that laboure and are laden and I wyll ease you.

He ignored the *Bishop's Bible* altogether. Developing a kind of method, with the swiftness and precision that comes with repeat performances, he turned to the translator's draft, which was, once again, spelling aside, identical to the octavo.

> Come unto me all yee that labour, and are laden and I will ease you.

As much as he wanted to leave it alone, as effortless as it was in his mouth, and as effortless as he expected it to be in the King's mouth, the line did not satisfy. A certain gravity was missing, or to his ear it was. "I will ease you" seemed a bit light for the task. He read the verse in its fullness, as it was.

> Come vnto me all yee that labour, and are laden, and I will ease you. Take my yoke vpon you, and learne of me, for I am meeke and lowly in heart: and yee shall find rest vnto your soules. For my yoke is easie, and my burden is light.

He thought how handsome the English was, with what ease and delicacy, and yet with what highness it read. Taking the cue from the line that followed, he reconstructed the troubling phrase. He also added a single modifier to soften the alliteration. It now read:

> Come vnto me all yee that labour, and are heavy laden, and I will ~~ease you~~ give you rest. Take my yoke vpon you, and learne of me, for I am meeke and lowly in

heart: and yee shall find rest vnto your soules. For my
yoke is easie, and my burden is light.

It's not that the translators were wrong, because they (and
Tyndale) had gotten it right. But the line now read with a music
it formerly lacked. It had both backbone and delicacy, not an
easy thing to achieve in a text. This was, indeed, what the King
had hired him for. He was ecstatic in the change, and for the
first time he understood the justice of his anonymity. His name
would get in the way. He was playing the role he had rehearsed
all his professional life, the ghost.

"A goodly king, and a wise," he thought to himself.

He was ready to proceed at tempo.

"Like the facility with which you do your work, you are quite
unassuming," the King said to the Poet one afternoon late.
"Forgive our candor, but you seem not to carry the weight about
your person that your work does." His words were gentle, as was
the Poet's reply.

"I am an uncomplicated man, Majestie."

"Now you trifle with your king."

"I am a craftsman, Majestie, like my father. I work with my
hands."

"You toy with us. A craftsman built this palace, laid the
stones beneath us, fitted the joints on these chairs you see here,
and indeed, these are fine pieces of work. Our shoes, the care and
delicacy, yes, these are the work of a craftsman, but . . ." He had
the Poet lead him to the fireplace. "'There is witchcraft in your

hands,'" the King added. The pause leaned favorably toward the Poet, and he left it in the power of the King. "We understand your humility," the King continued, "but you do yourself disparagement. Our bible will be the soul of the reign, ah, but yours . . . yours is the voice it will be remembered by." The King paused as he considered his next words. "A power greater than our own, greater than all kings and kingdoms has brought you here."

The King seemed taller, straighter as he spoke. The fire blazing hot and golden behind him enhanced the image. The King then shifted downward with his next words, in a tone more confessional than conversational. "I never knew my father. He suffered a fate I might have suffered many times had Divinity not spared me. My mother was taken from me before I was a year old. The Virgin queen saw to her death many years later, and . . ." A confusion thicker than his tongue resurrected the dead queens. "We committed the worst of crimes, against nature itself, with our silence."

The Poet was mute. The King was speaking privately, perhaps things he had not spoken of at all before, sidestepping the royal *we* on occasion. The Poet had crept into royal favor, and though he would not question it, he knew it could be a dangerous place to stand. He said nothing. He was playing the confessor now. His gentleness and ease of manner, his delicacy with language, as well as his invisibility, charmed intimate speech from the King.

He heard the music again. And again, it was muted, distant, almost ghostlike, so much so he wondered if it had been playing the whole time, for it had that effect. He opened his mouth as if to ask the King about it but said nothing. It continued to play behind and around the two men.

The King was sober, his speech soft and low, speaking, as he was, somewhat underneath the Poet. In the warm space between them, the King was making his own judgments. He understood Francis Bacon's affinity for Will Shakespeare. And Jonson's envy. He understood why Southampton, even against a relationship turned sour, still commended the Poet to his world.

The Poet was secretly glad for the closing of the playhouses. It gave him time to think, to consider his options, to put distance between himself and the lash that had driven him for twenty years. His compensation by the Crown was more than sufficient to answer for the loss. He turned to the Bishop's Bible and read the first few passages aloud.

> Euery thyng hath a tyme, yea all that is vnder the heauen hath his conuenient season. There is a tyme to be borne, and a tyme to dye: there is a tyme to plant, and a tyme to plucke vp the thyng that is planted. A tyme to slay, and a tyme to make whole: a tyme to breake downe, and a tyme to builde vp. A tyme to weepe, and a tyme to laugh: a tyme to mourne, & a tyme to daunce . . .

He turned to Coverdale, which, other than the spelling, started in the same dull pedestrian manner. "Every thinge hath a tyme, yee all that is vnder the heauen hath . . ." Having long cultivated an ear for recognizing a text that needed work from the first reading, this was one of them.

He turned to Wycliffe again. He didn't expect to take

anything from it but amusement. He read the passage, and though he smiled, he was no closer to any resolve than when he started. "Alle thingis han tyme," it read, "and alle thingis undur sunne passen bi her spaces." As much as he loved Wycliffe, meaning or musical sense was vacant. He turned to the translator's draft and for the first time saw what this verse might become. The opening construction, with the preposition *to* pleased his ear.

> To everything there is a time . . . and under heaven a season for every purpose.

Once again, he wasn't sure with what severity he may be tampering with the Hebrew, but he made a few marks on the page and read it again.

> To everything there is a ~~time~~ season, and under heaven a ~~season~~ time for every purpose.

Not completely certain of its present state, and thinking it best to pause, he stood upright, then stepped out of the room. He walked past the guard in the direction he thought the music might be coming from. The guard followed maybe two meters behind him and in full military step. The volume never seemed to change but remained constant wherever he was in the palace. He turned and asked where the music was coming from. The guard said nothing but remained at attention. After a few minutes, the Poet returned to the chamber and resumed his posture over the books. The music continued to play. There were times it felt so close to him he thought he might touch it.

He took his pen, and quickly made alterations to the line, and read it again.

> To everything there is a ~~time~~ season, and ~~under heaven~~ a ~~season~~ time for every purpose under heaven ~~every purpose~~.

For the joy he felt, he might have danced there at the table, but with Henry VII staring at him as stupidly as he was, he thought better of the impulse. And he wasn't sure he had the leg for it anymore. The parallel construction that followed in verses 2 through 8 was honeysweet to his ear—the drone, the sobriety, the tallness, the solemn drum beating beneath it all.

Unnoticed, the octavo was back in his hands again. When his father died, he carried his father's old missal in the same manner, printed in octavo and for the same reasons. It too was contraband. But it was his father's, and though he found questionable solace in its content, there was a time he was never without it. Unknown by the King, though suspected by Cecil, his family was old world catholic, as many in Stratford-Upon-Avon remained. After being warned by Francis Bacon about seizure, he decided to keep his father's old book in a trunk.

With the octavo in his hand, he wondered why the King and Richard Bancroft decided to use the Bishop's Bible at all, much less as the baseline or default translation. The more he scanned the Bishop's Bible the more absurd it seemed that it was even on the table. The octavo was master here.

CHAPTER SEVEN

Hamlet and Horatio

AT THE CHANGING OF THE REIGNS, LONDON was a bustling though compact world with a population of about two-hundred thousand, give or take an outbreak of Bubonic plague, war with Spain, or the lynching queues at Tyburn or Smithfield. To keep a secret in such a compressed space was not easy. Tongues were swift, imaginations were reckless and ill-informed, and there were eyes and ears everywhere—in the walls, in the woodwork, in the air (unless you were thrown off by the smell). Sermons at St. Paul's could be a real test of one's faith considering the burial grounds just outside and the ripeness of its tenants.

In the sixth year of the new king, Francis Bacon walked with the Poet one midsummer afternoon near the bookstalls in Paul's churchyard. Engaged in some mutual distraction of thought concerning the philosophical pitfalls of blank verse, they were suddenly assaulted by a foulness impossible to ignore, describe, or avoid, downwind as they were.

"These are reeky times, Will," the Philosopher said. The joke was old by 1609, but for the sake of his friend and the prompt that lay unanswered, the Poet returned in kind.

"And the Scot has the most advanced rank in the kingdom." The slander was small, and though it lacked conviction it made him uncomfortable. "Francis, I need to ask you something."

"Anything, sweet melancholy."

"There is an old octavo at Richmond."

"Like the one in your hand?"

"It is a true wonder for its size. Grand," he said, not wanting to overstate his modifiers. "Outspeaks all the others on the table."

"May I see it?" The Poet handed Francis the book. "So what is the issue?"

"It has no author, chuck, or seems it so."

"Is there no inscription in the front matter, a printer's stamp, city, a date?"

Bacon took the octavo from his friend and read aloud.

The Newe Testament as it was written, and caused to be written, by them which herde yt. To whom also oure saveoure Christe Iesu commanded that they shulde preache it unto al creatures . . .

"William Tyndale," the Philosopher said plainly, "Or Hitchens," he added, returning the book to the Poet. "That's the man."

"William Tyndale? Or Hitchens? That's the man?"

"Of Gloucestershire, near the border of Wales if Foxe is reliable."

"From the midlands?"

"Like yourself, Will."

"William Tyndale?" Saying the name seemed to legitimize it, made it real to him.

"It is a remarkable piece of history," the Philosopher said, distracted by a hawk overhead.

"I am under orders to take nothing from the palace."

"And yet I see you've grown attached."

"I'll put it back. William Tyndale, you say?"

"That is precisely why it is small, my melodious felon. It was a smuggled book, an outlawed book, contraband." Francis often dramatized his speech with some rhetorical spur, though he would not consider it art.

"Of Gloucestershire? A midlander you say?"

"It was a matter of concealment."

"This fellow has a marvelous fine ear."

"It had to be small enough to hide in a cloak."

"On or about the border of Wales?"

"Or a crate of tobacco, or tea perhaps, even cloth."

"Tyndale, you say?"

"What vexes thee, that you reiterate so upon the poor man's name?"

"This octavo . . . is become my delight."

"You speak in pentameter, so I know thou art sincere, but please do not say his name again."

"Why, Francis, did I not know this poet?"

"You have Sir Thomas More to thank for that. More would

have had the poor man expunged, erased, plucked altogether from the memory of this country. For More and others, Tyndale was the most hated and feared man in the realm, at least among More's kind. In all the world really. He was more despised than the Saxon."

"The Saxon?"

"Dr. Luther."

"Why did More hate the translator so much?"

"He wasn't . . . papal. He was earnest. He was resolute. He was brilliant and focused. He was even accused of doing some fine preaching, and, oddly, by More himself. He just wasn't Roman. More had spies everywhere. He had the backing of the Pope. With the bounty on the poor man's head, we should be surprised Tyndale lived long enough to produce anything."

"But he did, Francis. Quite notably too."

"Your blank verse is annoying."

If it was an age of foul smell, and it was, it was also an age of rumor. As important as it was to the King to keep the Poet's involvement in the translation private, in such a confined space as the city was, as the court was, or the theatres, and being the pipe rumor is, it could not be done. As pungent as the times could be, Ben Jonson had wind of something. He always had his nose in the air. Because the Poet stayed in or around the city during seasons of plague, Jonson chose to remain in town as well. He was not unaware of the Poet's continuing presence at Hampton Court, which, as rumor can often be, was ill-informed. Outside the few plays performed there, the Poet was most often at Richmond.

Shakespeare had a way of vexing the bully playwright like no one else could. Any hint of favor or advancement given to Will Shakespeare, every applause, every elevated opinion, every positive review vexed him. His chubby laughter vexed him. It is not possible to exhaust the word when it came to Jonson's rancor toward the Poet.

Jonson had the great good fortune to come under the patronage of Robert Cecil, who was, at that time the most powerful man in the kingdom (next to the King, of course), and the richest. The patronage was not an aesthetic consideration for Cecil, as the appointment may have implied or as Jonson convinced himself. It was politic. With Cecil, everything was politic. It was the art he cherished. He had no other thought in his mind.

Cecil harbored a grievance against the Poet as well. But however small or large the grievance, Cecil knew better than to reveal anything to Jonson about the King's commission. He was afraid, and rightly so, that Jonson would do something crude and primitive, and worse, public, in response.

But dangerous men have their uses.

Robert Cecil, also known as the Earl of Salisbury, had seen many plays of the Poet. Shakespeare was the "thing" after all. Southampton had declared it, as did most of London after him. As busy as Cecil was, and as occupied with rumor (whether gathering or initiating), he was obligated to attend court performances, which were on the increase. He respected the Poet, but was, himself, unpoetical. Truth is, there was no soul more unpoetical than Robert Cecil. He never grew warm to ballad-making, bombast, or any of the usual charms of the age, though he did enjoy an occasional bear-baiting.

Cecil particularly disliked RICHARD III. His resemblance to the hunchbacked king was unsettling. The black outfit, the lute shaped back, the lethal slime that coated his words, was uncomfortable for Robert to watch, and indeed, he suffered insult in the fallout of that play. The Poet captured not only Cecil's appearance, but his word constructions, his tone, the very shape and nature of his schemes.

The Poet could unsettle the bent little man like few in the Kingdom.

RICHARD III was written and performed in 1592 not long after Essex was made a member of the Privy Council. Robert Cecil was sport for the Essex tribe, and RICHARD III didn't help. The Poet provided an arsenal for their cruelties.

That bottled spider, that poisonous bunchback'd toad.

Thou lump of foul deformity.

Thou elvish-mark'd, abortive, rooting hog!

Slinging mud has been a part of political ordnance since primitive man first learned to compete with primitive man on the public stage, and Cecil most often let it roll off his misshapen back. But the insult that made the deepest cut and widened the breach between him and the Poet was not even verbal. It was of a more mundane stripe, as to appear almost innocuous to the casual observer, but it identified Cecil as the model for the loathsome prince. Cecil rarely betrayed emotion, but when unduly stressed he was known to bite his lip. It was the Poet's greatest offense.

The king is angry: see, he bites the lip.

But Lord Robert was patient. His father had taught him to be patient. He had little choice but to be patient, and he always came out on top. By 1601, the Earl of Essex's head was on the block. Of course, in all fairness, Essex needed little help from Cecil, being as the Earl was, the architect of his own tragic end.

RICHARD III was not the only injury the First Minister suffered at the hands of the Poet. Being at the receiving end of heartless jest all his life, OTHELLO's Iago stung him grievously, with a subtlety and craft still green in the Poet's RICHARD III. The duplicity, the finesse, the charm by which he moved among them all, the blackness of his costume and his spirit, the general slither and dominion he maintained throughout the play, including his captaincy over the captain, was too much for Cecil to take. He felt exposed. Iago was a comic villain, which only compounded the offense, and made the private joke all the more powerful for those who got it.

Francis Bacon, who missed nothing, admired the audacity of his friend's genius, though at times he could not help but feel a touch of ice on his flesh. He knew Cecil had genius of his own, that he was an artist of a kind, even a poet beneath a certain dark light. Offended as Cecil was, he was privately amused, if not remotely flattered by Iago, Richard, and the many other ghosts of his image the Poet called to life under his hands. He would wait.

The Poet felt that if he could not improve Tyndale, if he could not make Tyndale's work shine with an even greater brilliance than it did on its own as the translators had labored to do, or enhance the beauty already evident in the text, he chose to leave it alone. For him, it wasn't about accuracy or submitting to the original transmission. Let the translators sweat the Greek and the Hebrew. His ear was tuned to the English. Except for a single word, and the spelling, the translator's draft and the octavo were once again identical.

> For the word of God is quicke and mighty in operacion, and sharper then any two edged sword and entereth through euen to the diuiding asunder of soule and spirit, and of the ioynts and marrowe, and is a discerner of the thoughts and intents of the heart.

He spoke the line out loud as habit dictated. It had the effect of a powerful lyric but to his ear it had a limited vitality. Careful not to obscure meaning, he considered two bold but simple changes.

Substituting the single word *powerfull* for *mighty in operacion*, he exchanged eight syllables for three. The compression read smoothly to his ear and allowed no interruption in the line. In the same fashion, and taking his cue from the *Wycliffe Bible* ('*and more able to perse than any tweyne eggid swerd*'), he substituted *pearcing* for *entereth through*, two syllables for four. He felt not only the economy of the line had improved but that his verbs of choice were stronger in both instances, evoking drama and movement, giving it a poetic impact that Tyndale's *entereth through* seemed to deny, sterile as it was to him. Plus, he liked the sound of it. The final, or amended version appeared thus:

For the word of God is quicke and ~~mighty in operacion~~
powerfull, and sharper then any two edged sword, ~~and
entereth through~~ pearcing euen to the diuiding asun-
der of soule and spirit, and of the ioynts and marrowe,
and is a discerner of the thoughts and intents of the
heart.

In spite of any changes he made, and the faith it took to
make them, his awe for the martyred translator suffered no loss.
Tyndale was beautiful, after all. Some things would not be improved upon. He came to esteem the name as only a poet, or at
least one of equal stature could. Like himself, here was no me-
chanic, no counterfeit or mimic, but an English original. He was
certain his dead cousin, Robert Southwell, would have approved
the manner in which Tyndale used his poetic gifts.

He shuddered as if brushed by an apparition.

Whether out of curiosity, boredom, or to circumnavigate dull
routine, he vacillated between the Old and New Testaments,
working in equal measures between them. While the King had
been present in the early stages, approving, offering commentary, or simply exercising nervous curiosity, by mid 1609 His
Majestie hardly came around anymore, busy as he was with affairs of state, or some new favorite.

"You have no more use of us Master Shakespeare," the King
said at last. "We will prove impediment." His manner was agreeable and warm, as it had been since their first encounter. Though
the Poet understood the King, he had looked forward to the

sound of His Majestie ambling through the great hall, the uneven tap and stutter of his gait, the thick Scots by which he most
often shaped his words, the sad droop of his eyes.

He thought to himself how unfair his judgments had been
toward the King, and how there was, like himself, much more
to James than his outward show could possibly betray. In spite
of his royal opinion making, his need to impose his wit, or
the way he could mesmerize the Poet with his odd humanity,
however fond the image, in the year and a half Shakespeare
worked on the translation, he and the King had only one real
disagreement.

Francis Bacon was the one person the Poet trusted when he
sought opinion on a text. His Greek was unparalleled, comparable only to Henry Savile. Bacon was the only council the Poet
sought if he sought council at all.

"The King is immovable?"

"He will not be persuaded."

"Remember, Will, this is a royal enterprise. The King's consideration is political, magisterial." The Poet stared back without
speech. Bacon continued. "Don't look so undone. It is a matter of good government. Cecil would applaud the King for his
insistence. And you have to give it to him. His Greek does not
suffer, in spite of how it bends on occasion for His Majestie. But
for him, *charity* is the better choice, the wiser choice. *Charity* is
a royal word, a magnanimous word. A monarch can be charitable, and that show of charity elevates him in the eyes of his
people. But love? Love is a bit more obscure from such a height.
Charity? Charity is tangible. It is a politically expedient word,
my duck. It implies a gift, a benefit, some endowment from
the Crown. He wants them to think majestie, highness, royal

beneficence. In truth, that's the only reason he bothers at all with a new translation. This enterprise is not about art. Nor is it spiritual, as it might pretend. It is pure statecraft. He wants the Englishman to read the lines as if each one were cast with his royal image, like a minted coin." He took every advantage of the pause, then spoke again. "The first epistle of John? Is God *love* or is he *charity*?"

"God is love."

"Put your argument to rest, Will. From what you tell me, he has offered very little resistance to your alterations. If it helps His Majestie to sleep better at night, if he sleeps, my advice is to let it go. Everyone is the happier." His tone lightened. "I say 'Put money in thy purse.'" The Poet laughed at the reference, caught off guard as he was. "Go about thy business, enjoy the King's favor, fulfill your commission, make your mark in this little history, and . . . 'Put money in thy purse.' Do the work asked of thee. Be of good cheer. Take two steps backward and . . . 'Put money in thy purse.'" Francis Bacon was the one man in the kingdom who had the ability to deepen the laughter of the Poet, bound as they were, soul to soul.

Robert Cecil, though he had learned to bury an insult, felt the cut of the Poet's caricatures and burned inwardly for it nonetheless. Unwittingly, and with good humor the Poet became a woodcock to his own springe, as he might have said it himself. He was on the dark side of Cecil's favor, and once in the disfavor of Salisbury there is no talking one's way out. But the Poet could not help himself. As a dramatist, as an artist, he found

inspiration where it was to be found and cultivated it. He plagiarized all life around him. It was rarely personal. He took what
he wanted from whomever he wanted and amplified, distorted,
stretched, and altered it until satisfied.

Ben Jonson could not have delighted more to know that his
rival held such displeasure and kept such a cold place in Lord
Robert's heart. It was a powerful physick to know that another
soul was as vexed toward the Poet as he. Jonson was loud. His
slander was loud. There was self-flattery in the derision.

Cecil, however, was careful to remain inconspicuous. He
was not of the blunt-instrument-quick-to-speak-slow-to-listen
school Jonson was. His pounce was studied, calculated. He had
more restraint than any man in the kingdom. And better timing. He indeed bit his lip on occasion, but as a rule he had no
tell. An insult never effected the first change in his aspect, not
one facial muscle. He chose instead, by his father's tutelage, to
record the insult, to call it back in a more propitious time. An
adversary would be fallen and outcast before he even knew he
was stung. Essex understood all too late what this meant. Sir
Walter Raleigh was ruined by Cecil's smiling duplicity. The little
man, having received passionate letters from the desperate and
Tower-bound Raleigh, replied with small allotments of hope,
empty as they were, to the unsuspecting and soon-to-be head-
less ex-pirate.

Robert Cecil was of the vengeance-is-a-dish-best-served-
cold school of justice, and Iago was an insult. As precise as it was,
it was a greater offense than any laid to the charge of Essex or
Southampton. It was by the hand of the Poet himself, who chose
to cast Cecil's image in a comic light, a caricature, a buffoon, a
slithering little villain dressed in black, silenced at the end but

only after destroying the very world he had office in. Again, he would wait.

⚜

The translation, though not a secret, kept a low profile nonetheless, or as low as it could considering how porous and compact the London social circles. There was no buzz on either campus as might be expected. Bishops were not yet demanded to argue on its behalf from the pulpits. With many such innovations and changes initiated with the new reign, all the high speeches, all the empty air, it went unnoticed.

The Puritans were pacified for the moment too, though you could not say they were happy.

Francis Bacon's driving energies toward scientific investigation were influenced greatly by the Poet's ardor for new shapes in language, new geometries, movement, and textures of English. The King was not unaware of the bond between them. He was content in the match knowing his new Bible was in the most capable of hands.

"Have you considered leaving your signature, Will?"

"What do you mean, Francis?"

"In the text, some covert mark below the surface, out of the direct light so to speak, something that identifies you, that says you were here, something beyond detection." The wit of Francis Bacon was perspicacious, as round as it was deep. "You should consider it. Who can conceal an object better than you?"

"What a tragedian you would have made."

"To-tus mun-dus a-git his-tri-o-nem."[18]

"And in pentameter."

"I'm afraid you have the wrong Bacon."

Though he died the year HAMLET was staged, Anthony Bacon, if not abroad, was usually at the Essex House, where he had a room of his own. Never short on tales of his travels, and never too shy to tell them—Verona, Milan, Naples, Venice, Athens, Paris, Rome—brother Anthony always had about him a small crowd, the Poet being the most attentive among them, and with the deepest ear.

Anthony's verbal gifts were as replete as his more famous brother, and he was a bit of a playwright himself. His descriptions of the cities and adjacent countryside were lucid, and framed in the finest constructions the language and the age could afford. His powers of observation were as skilled as any poet of worth. Having nurtured his own appreciation for the Poet, Anthony spent many hours of conversation with him. He commented to Francis once about the Poet's penetrating curiosity, his dedication to his craft. He mentioned also the ease in which he seemed to conceal, if not dissemble, such a talent. The Poet was hardly aware that he was caught in some intellectual gulf between the brothers. Francis recognized his brother's spirit in the melancholy Antonio in THE MERCHANT OF VENICE. He thought it a fine tribute.

The conversation continued.

"Some impression of my name, you mean, buried in the text?" The question nodded favorably in his thoughts.

"What a man of law you would make, Will. You could make your great speeches, and toy with all the delicate algebra of your arguments . . . aim the great arrow of your wit in defense of Lady Justice."

"I assure you the stage is all the courts of law, all the pulpit I need, Francis. Besides, who can stand up against you in a courtroom? I have seen the poor sods drown in their own sweat, choking on Justice as she plays the maid to your advances. I have watched the whole court suspend on your every word, to hang there upon your tale as if it would cure deafness itself." The Philosopher was distracted by two dogs that ran by them in a hurry. "I've seen them balance upon the leanest alteration of your speech, every fall and every rise of emotion," the Poet continued, his hyperbole warm. "When you clear your throat, a man faints for want of strength. When you beat a man, he doesn't recover. When you expose him, he is marked for life. When a man falls on my stage, he is in his cups one hour after, ready to fall again the next afternoon. No, no, you, Francis, you are the wit. I am . . . the dissembler, the prince of fancy."

"And anyway, I would have thought so," Bacon said, as if he had heard not the slightest word.

"Thought what?" said the Poet's annoyed Horatio to Bacon's distracted Hamlet.

"I mean it is all so Walsingham and Burghley isn't it? So very spymaster? So many secrets and so few mouths to rattle them in. I was sure you might have considered it. Anonymity with a gift as large as yours cannot be easy. Nor should it be tolerated."

"I have not been given sanction by the King to leave any such mark."

"But you have been given no sanction against it. And when did such a thing ever stand in your way? Your Scottish play took aim at the royal bugger, and in his own house." The Poet smiled at the report. "You hurled that needle-sharp tip of your fancy into the ruffle of the King's mind. Anyone else would have been thrown in the Tower. I thought he would run from the palace or piss himself."

Both men laughed.

"It would have to be submerged in the text, of course," the Poet said.

"I imagine he crammed more of Andrewes's sermons under his pillow," said the Philosopher.

"Outside detection," the Poet continued, "from the Crown, from the directors, and from Cecil." He lost concentration when the same two dogs ran by them going in the opposite direction.

CHAPTER EIGHT

Beauty in the Mouth of a Monster is Always Unsettling

THE IMPATIENCE OF A KING IS UNLIKE THE IMPATIENCE OF OTHER MEN. Even so, strung as tightly as he is, with or without a crown James can do up to five things at once without losing focus or tempo. And though His Majestie marvels at the speed with which his servant, the soon-to-be Sir William, has sifted the old text line by line, the Poet can hear the royal toe tapping in the background.

Producing a minimum of two plays per year, in or out of plague, the Poet is accustomed to rapid output. There are only a few issues left. The changes he has made are so subtle, the music so refined, with the exception of John Bois and a select few, it is doubtful the translators will even notice. After so much time and labor without recompense, they are ready for an end as well.

Toward the end of 1608, James commanded Edmund Tylney, Master of the Revels, to close the playhouses. Plague or the possibility of plague was all the excuse he needed to give the Poet the latitude and time necessary to complete his commission. Plague is also a fertile time for playwriting, but he has been so consumed with the translation, so determined to please the King, and so taken with the glittering new world he has been invited into, he thinks little of the playhouse. And there is no theater as grand as royalty itself.

There were times he wished he had never accepted the King's commission.

Other times he wished it would never end.

When away from Richmond he continued to write, but the great fire in him belonged to the Crown. After ANTONY AND CLEOPATRA from 1608 to 1610, each successive play possessed less sparkle than the one preceding it—CYMBELINE, PERICLES, TIMON OF ATHENS, like a comfortable pair of slippers he returned to old themes, old forms. CORIOLANUS had its moments. With the bread shortage in London the play at least had topical elements. THE WINTER'S TALE showed signs of his earlier successes.

It bewildered him how much he enjoyed the work. The time sped by quickly. On most days, other than a guard, there was not a soul around, just the old books, the portraits on the wall, the lush furnishings, and a generous view of the Thames.

As he idled, the music began to play again, in muted tones all around him. He thought little of it and opened the translator's draft once again to the stubborn passage in 1 Kings. There was something he wasn't hearing and it wasn't in him to turn the other cheek. He repeated the words to himself.

. . . and after the winde an earthquake, but the Lord
was not in the earthquake. And after the earthquake, a
fire, but the Lord was not in the fire: and after the fire,
a small still voice.

Of the literally hundreds of lines he had altered so far, this
was the one single itch he could not scratch. He walked over to
the window. Having spent months in this one room, he could
walk about blindfolded. He tripped against the table nonetheless, and laughed at himself, stumped as he was by the passage
in question.

It was raining as hard as he had seen it rain in a while. But far
from dousing his spirits, he was swept up in the fascination—the
gray gloom of the river, a moaning in the wind, thunder rattling
a saber over London. The music playing quietly beneath it all.

He sang quietly to himself. *Take, Oh, take those lips away,
that so sweetly were forsworn.* He had little use for theology. He
had seen too many lives undone for the sake of belief. He admired scripture, even loved it in his way, if only for its voice, its
profound sea-floor hush, and the occasional aria.

What few alterations he made to the Psalms were of a quiet
nature. *And those eyes, the break of day, Lights that do mislead the
morn.* He applied a spare, even justice—a word here, a two or
three-word phrase there, a transposition, a deletion. He stalled
many times before the old hymns, sometimes out of mild frus-
tration with a sound, other times just to listen. Its old music, the
familiar comforts. *But my kisses bring again, bring again; Seals of
love but sealed in vain, sealed in vain.*

Whole days passed. He had been known to brood for long
hours, at times over a single passage, not for any meditative

consideration, but for sound, for the music it makes or refuses to make. That is the argument, he reminds himself.

Of all the Psalms, 137 moved him the most, with its loss, its groan of memory, the cleft it makes in the heart. His children had grown up without him. His wife, abandoned young, a theater widow, had grown shrewish with age and her husband's absence. His son (Hamnet) and father (John) having died while he was away, he could not read the words without a sting of regret or something like regret.

> By the riuers of Babylon, there wee sate downe, yea we wept: when we remembred Zion. We hanged our harpes upon the willows . . .

The words struggled in him, but not for sound. 137 was one of several he did not touch.

> How shall we sing the Lords song in a strange land? If I forget thee, O Ierusalem: let my right hand forget her cunning. If I doe not remember thee, let my tongue cleaue to the roofe of my mouth; if I preferre not Ierusalem aboue my chiefe ioy.

By old habit, as from any text he admired, he borrowed. In Richard II a trembling Aumerle swears before Bolingbroke, now Henry IV:

> For ever may my knees grow to the earth,
> My tongue cleave to my roof within my mouth
> Unless a pardon ere I rise or speak.

In spite of its 176 verses, he made only two changes to Psalm 119. Verse 105 in the translator's draft followed the stout but pitiably unimaginative Bishop's Bible, which read:

Thy worde is a candell vnto my feete: and a light vnto my path.

The change he made was swift and righteous. With a few marks he read it again.

Thy worde is a ~~candell~~ lampe unto my feete: and a light unto my path.

"A lamp unto my feet" made the better music. It wasn't the parallel construction or the alliteration. It simply pleased his ear. He wondered how the translators could miss something so conspicuous. Satisfied, he reread 119 for the pleasure of it, only to stumble at verse 11.

I haue hid thy promes in mine heart, that I might not sinne against thee.

With verse 105 still warm on his lips, he made an alteration to this verse as well, for the sake of consistency, the grand whole.

~~I haue hid~~ Thy ~~promes~~ worde haue I hid in mine heart, that I might not sinne against thee.

When the King saw these changes, he almost wept. When he had speech, he said, "For the sake of a single word, the apt word . . . marvelous." Having chosen the apt word himself, the King then repeated it for effect. "Marvelous," he said again. He then turned and waddled slowly out of the chamber.

For all the beauty of Job the book, the Poet could not understand Job the person at all. To have the ear of God and to suffer as he did and with such eloquence made no sense to him. He thought Job a fool, though, like many of his own fools, possessed with a lovely voice.

> My dayes are swifter then a weauers shuttle, and are spent without hope. O remember that my life is winde: mine eye shall no more see good. The eye of him that hath seene me, shall see mee no more: thine eyes are vpon me, and I am not. As the cloud is consumed and vanisheth away: so he that goeth downe to the graue, shall come vp no more. Hee shall returne no more to his house: neither shall his place know him any more. Therefore I will not refraine my mouth, I wil speake in the anguish of my spirit, I will complaine in the bitternesse of my soule.

My dayes are swifter than a weaver's shuttle . . . He admired the line, its gravity and movement. But for all its beauty, and the minor key it was written in, the remainder of the passage just seemed to whine, or it did to him—convincingly, of course. He thought of his Macbeth. "*My way of life has fall'n into the sear, the yellow leaf.*"[19]

Like the current weather, the Poet's mind was a broil of contending elements. He knew he was changing. He knew life was saying new things to him now, giving him new instructions. He stared at the translator's draft. He wasn't sure how or when it may have started, but he suspected the words before him were sifting him as much as he ever sifted them, and there was no undoing their strange magic.

In this humor, his cousin's ghost returned. Not only that, it seemed to smile upon him, which can be unsettling in a ghost. The Poet did not smile back. The ghost had the last word it seems, for the Poet was exercising his talents in service of not just the King, but the King of Kings, as the wily Southwell had exhorted him and poets like him many years before.

The only thing worse than a fine memory might be a meddling inner monologue.

He wondered how many more plays he had in him. Did he even care? He once cared very much. He was insatiable when it came to reading, and just as insatiable, if not ruthlessly predatorial, when it came to chasing down a source. He had exhausted the Bacon family library, including works by both brothers. He thought Anthony the better writer of the two. He had read everything in Southampton's library, and most everything in the Earl of Pembroke's, having spent long hours in both. The more he fed, the more ravenous he became.

Now, at almost forty-six, his appetites were in a state of flux. He began to tire of the playhouse the way one might tire of a beloved mistress who's grown old, fat, or tedious. His plays were beginning to reflect the decline. Perhaps it was the pride he felt under the King's gaze, an elevated kind of pride (for there is nothing quite so powerful as the royal nod when aimed in your direction). His professional life had been a pleasant dream and the dream was approaching some state of epilogue.

He was obligated to write at least one more play, and it was prudent that he do so. He owed his partners and himself that much. Like him, they were all older, a bit rounder, some balder, and certainly richer for his efforts.

It started coming to him, not in a downpour as the rain outside might have suggested, but by drip and drizzle, the pace of a fat man walking uphill. Because of the rain, the general gloom and candlelight, because of the music that played continuously in the air about the palace, it created in him a dreamlike state that allowed his muse to labor.

An exile of a kind, he looked about and imagined himself on an island, a remote outpost far from the common and familiar. Whether an Eden or a Patmos, it was enchanted—exotic woods, strange-fruited trees, lush foliage, a light mist on the ground, and music playing nearby almost imperceptibly in the atmosphere.

The play, he thought, would orbit around a central figure, a banished duke perhaps (As You Like It), who loves his books (Measure for Measure, Love's Labours Lost) and has a daughter (As You Like It, Merchant of Venice, King Lear, et al). Susanna will be in London soon. She married well, a doctor. Magic is another old theme that would work nicely (A Midsummer Nights Dream, Macbeth).

He began to add names as the first threads of a tale started coming together.

Mysterio, Duke of Perugia, banished by sibling treachery, has a second identity, that of sorcerer, conjurer, a wizard of sorts. By his magic arts, Mysterio creates a storm and causes the winds to howl while his daughter, Eugenia, sleeps. THE ISLAND, as he begins to call the play, opens with a shipwreck (TWELFTH NIGHT). The usurper brother (AS YOU LIKE IT) Licentio, is on the doomed ship along with others of his crew, those who have wronged the unwary, wise, charitable, but incautious Mysterio.

The names are place holders. They will change. Or they will not. It is his way.

It may have been the thought of returning home that shaped the final scene, calling back the familiar—a happy ending, a reconciliation, a marriage.

Stepping away from the table, he stared at its legs, footed as they were with a lion's paw, limbed by some unnamed sea thing. "A monster?" he said to no one. Obscene, dull-witted, half-man half-something else, something slithering. From the sea, of course.

Under Bacon's counsel the Poet had exhausted the essays of Montaigne, not in its original French, but through a translation by John Florio, a mutual friend of both Shakespeare and Bacon. With Montaigne still fresh in his memory, particularly an essay called "Of Cannibals," he gave his monster a name. "I dub thee Cannibal," he said. "I will write thee grand speeches, the finest in the play." Beauty in the mouth of a monster is always unsettling. And good for business (RICHARD III, MACBETH).

He took no notes, wrote nothing down. Possessing superb powers of retention, like his mother, Mary Arden Shakespeare, it had always been his practice to have the entire pageant in his head, to the smallest detail, including much of the dialogue, before committing anything to paper. It was an economic consideration. Paper wasn't cheap. His handwritten scripts were tidy that way.

By royal warrant, the Poet was commanded to restrain his use of witches. It didn't seem right, however, to have an enchanted island, a sorcerer, a crude, dull-witted, half-man, half-something else, and no witch. To appease the warrant and his imagination, he gives his fishified Cannibal a mother, a witch he names Kalypso, who is dead before the action begins. It is a daring move considering his royal audience.

As much as he tried to concentrate on the scripture before him, it seemed impossible. Once a play began to seep into his thought life there was little room for anything else, the cast half-formed and clamoring about his brains with little direction.

The draft was open to the book of Isaiah, Chapter 29. Though he read the passage out loud, the rain was coming down so hard, hissing and whistling against the great windows, he could hardly hear his own voice.

"Woe to Ariel!" he cried. "Yet I will distresse Ariel, and there shalbe heauinesse and sorrow . . ." The name grew on him quickly, one of the few names that made it to the final draft. Not to mimic MIDSUMMER too conspicuously, but the creation of another Puck was attractive to him. To his banished duke, a daughter, a nasty storm, a shipwreck, a dead witch, a usurper brother, and an obscene slithering man-beast, he added a puckish sprite he would call Ariel, who, like his predecessor, will be Mysterio's sleight of hand, the magic in the hat.

"You come in woe, my sprite, as it says right here in the old book. A curse lies upon thee, from the dead Kalypso, who has bound thee in stone. Or in waters, a tree, something. I,

Mysterio, will emancipate thee," the Poet said. "When time shall serve, of course."

He turned to the portrait of Henry VII on the wall and spoke to it. "Does that please you, Majestie?" He leaned toward the droll and dead Harry but there was no response. "You are too wise, your Grace. I suppose it could use . . . something."

He walked to the window again and listened to the rain. He knows it's a middling effort, a crude start haunted by ghosts of his former successes, that he plagiarizes himself shamelessly. He also knows a few fine speeches will clothe the fault.

Ben Jonson was at the Mermaid early for a Monday. With the playhouses closed and his muse afraid to go near him when aggravated, he medicated his idleness with a copious amount of sack. He didn't necessarily have to be in his cups to start bleating loudly and boldly, and unless you knew him it was difficult to tell one way or another. No one in the tavern could ignore him, though many tried.

He lost contact with Shakespeare. And his antenna was erect.

He got nothing out of Francis Bacon, who was uncomfortable around the man. Francis may have had a fondness for tavern banter, he may even have a measure of respect for the man's talent, but he always did his best not to engage with the brawl playwright if he didn't have to. It was his rule to avoid Jonson when possible. He hardly ever spoke to him directly, but circumspectly, in riddles that made the top-heavy playwright work for an answer, if there indeed was an answer. It didn't matter. Jonson knew that if Bacon had no knowledge of the Poet's whereabouts, or refused to tell, there was one man in the kingdom who would.

Robert Cecil had the best "nose" in the kingdom. He anticipated Jonson's inquiry. He admired Jonson. He knew Jonson to have a pugnaciously analytical mind and an unforgiving ambition, that he could even be innovative on occasion. He also knew him to be slower and more predictable when compared to himself or to Will Shakespeare.

Jonson asked for a meeting with Cecil, who was at Whitehall overseeing the demolition of the old banqueting house. Cecil agreed. The bustle, the clamor of workmen, and the general appearance of enterprise would keep the meeting brief.

"Lord, Robert," the larger man said. Lord Robert said nothing. "I understand Shakespeare has some business with the King." Cecil knew this was sheer baiting on Jonson's part, and marveled how clumsy it was.

"Not that I am privy too."

Jonson said nothing. He stared at Cecil, hoping he might say more. But he did not.

"Forgive me, Lord Robert. With the theatres closed, I . . ."

"If you're referring to the masque the King has commissioned of your friend, what concern is that of yours?" He knew his words had a sharp tip.

"A masque, you say?"

"Do not trouble yourself, sir. At the request of Her Majestie, the King has commissioned a masque from Shakespeare."

"Is the Queen displeased with mine?"

"On the contrary. Her Majestie is so pleased, she wants more." The text suspended with optimism between them. "She never liked the French ambassador anyway," he laughed.

"I wouldn't take the King's censure too hard. I can only guess that you will be commissioned for another masque soon. If Her Majestie has her way, of course. The King will do anything, Master Jonson, pay any bounty within his means to keep Her Majestie . . . pacified." In spite of his contempt for Shakespeare, Cecil had no choice but to keep his involvement in the translation from Jonson. He knew even then that Jonson would end the life of the Poet someday.

"Now, I beg your leave, sir," Cecil said. "I have a pressing matter with Master Jones about the new banqueting hall."

"Of course," Jonson replied. He made a flourish and walked away. Later that night, after brooding for some time in a Cheapside tavern, he began walking toward Silver Street, toward the Mountjoy's.

"I will rid my soul of thee." The thought warmed him. At Muggle Street, within sight of Mountjoy's, he stopped and looked up at the sky. There was no moon or stars. The clouds were moving rapidly and angrily above him. He knew the storm was going to remain for days, coiled and aggravated as it was over London. But he didn't need a tortured sky to remind him what was in his soul.

At that moment, a carriage stopped in front of the tavern. At the sight of the Royal emblem on the door, his blood resumed its former boil that had just begun to cool. He knew Cecil had lied to him, but that was of little consequence at the moment.

He watched from the shadows.

His old friend and nemesis stepped out of the carriage with something in his hand—a box, a small book perhaps. The Poet said something to the driver and walked inside the tavern.

For all the spleen that had driven him that night, Jonson did nothing. He looked down at the dagger growling in his hand. He couldn't remember taking it out of its sheath. He put it back gently, turned and walked away.

It wasn't a night to kill a poet. It was too wet, too dark and stormy. No writer, he thought proudly to himself, should ever be murdered on such a night. He would wait.

CHAPTER NINE

I Do Adore the Little Bawd

Ben Jonson arrived at Hatfield House that morning just in time for the demolition of another wing. Construction was a preoccupation with the Cecils, a private fascination. It was not uncommon to see masons, carpenters, painters, gardeners, and other workmen engaged about the estate. Jonson's presence would go unnoticed. Cecil was standing under a canopy a reasonable distance from the house, leaning over a table making notes on what appeared to the playwright as architectural drawings of the doomed wing.

The bricks were to be preserved for the construction of a new Hatfield House, so, much of the work was accomplished by a slow and quiet method of deconstruction, brick by brick. Any powder used was set in small but strategic charges, and only as Cecil himself directed. If anyone knew the delicate algebra of power it was Robert Cecil, Earl of Salisbury—when and how much force to apply at a given moment, where to place the charge for a specific result.

"We have placed a charge here, here, and . . . here," he said to the playwright, pointing to different locations on the drawing in front of him. Having worked in masonry as a young man, Jonson gained a new respect for the First Minister. Cecil gave a nod to the workmen who lit the fuse then stepped away to a safe distance.

It was like muted thunder. Not a large blast, but a strategic one.

"Is it not interesting, Master Jonson, that with a judicious placement of powder, how easily a house falls?" His eyes never left the drawing as he spoke. The playwright was impressed with Cecil's grasp of metaphor, as disturbing as it was. "It's all in the arithmetic," he added. With calculations of his own, Jonson decided he would not like to be on the wrong side of Cecil's arithmetic. "The quieter method brings the most satisfaction," said the political strategist to the once bricklaying playwright.

Cecil never forgot an insult, however slight, or old. It was his practice to redress even the smallest of offenses, to clear all accounts, and with the same science he applied to the destruction of a great house, if not with comparable results. Francis Bacon's star was suppressed under the last administration, and refused to rise or shine. Bacon was coerced as well to prosecute the Earl of Essex, an unpopular role that neither he nor anyone else wanted. Cecil, the Philosopher's own cousin, was the chief architect behind that as well, though everyone looked to the Queen. The poor dumb dash of an earl had no chance, caught, as he was, between Cecil's dark genius and the Queen's wrath.

Blame never seemed to light on the little man.

"You would have made a marvelous tragedian, Lord Robert."

Dismissing the comment, Cecil asked, "The nature of your grievance?"

"He is insufferable. I do adore the little bawd, and will never weep so hard to do what I must."

"Listen carefully." Cecil was emphatic. "I want you to contain that great homicide I detect in you. What business the King has with Master Shakespeare is state business, and of no consequence to you. The playhouses will reopen soon. When they do, you will know that business is concluded. Even so, exercise patience. Do nothing. Bridle that monstrous pride of yours as well, and that famous temper." His words were gentle enough, but the intent behind them was not. Jonson said nothing, still looking in the direction of the toppled wing.

A servant appeared carrying a small but heavy wooden box and took it directly to Jonson. "Open it," Cecil instructed. Jonson turned the latch. There were one hundred new-minted Rose Ryal coins in the box. The gold caught what light there was. On top of the coins was a slip of paper with a man's name on it. "I believe you know the name. He has physick for you, medicines to cure your ills." Lord Robert took the slip of paper and held it over the candle and let it burn. "Mark me. Let the house come down gently, at low volume. Raise no dust in the fall. Do you understand?" The playwright understood it wasn't a request. He answered with an affirmative. "One more thing." Cecil paused. "Once you have satisfied your vengeance, find a way to praise the man." Before Jonson could protest or say anything, Cecil continued. "Give him your best words." Cecil could easily read the playwright's indecision and snapped at it. "Are you so dull, Master Jonson? Let your sorrow be loud but not overloud, your volume modest. Do you mark me?"

"By my troth, I . . ."

"Gild his image. Overlay it with gold. Modesty becomes revenge with much more satisfaction than violence, and with a gloss that hides the offense. Be prepared to take the lead in this enterprise. You'll see how right the device is, and how right you are for it. Take your time. Let your hyperbole weep, knowing with great satisfaction that which no one else knows, that you, Ben Jonson, sent him to his maker." Out of character, and before a delightfully bewildered Ben Jonson, Cecil actually laughed. His small belly shook. He then handed the playwright a small leather purse filled with gold coins. "Give this to Master Forman." Cecil then turned and resumed his business at the table. The playwright, duly unsettled, made a small show of reverence then went home much richer and wiser for his time.

The Poet hated the thought of leaving Richmond, that his time there was coming to an end. Richmond was a crown on his head. It provided a stage for him to dream on, a remote outpost to recover his soul again. And there is nothing sweeter than royal applause, the nod of grateful majestie. He could live with the anonymity.

As uneasy as he may have felt at the beginning, after so many months he was at peace with the ghosts that gathered in that little room—Henry VII, Elizabeth of York, the martyred Tyndale, his cousin the Jesuit, maybe even the ghost of his old life before the twins were born.

He never found out where the music came from, and stopped asking. Whether it was genuine or a product of his fancy, he chose not to speculate. But after Richmond, what was left? He would not be a spectator of his own decline. He loved London, the theater, and the life it gave him, the coin it put in his pocket, but he was not one to revel in old glories. Memories are short. He didn't mind a quiet departure. Not to mention that life in the city had gotten much younger. The players were younger, the poets, including those underling playwrights he was asked to take under his wing, the lusty souls determined to emulate his achievement or dethrone him. Burbage no longer made a convincing Romeo. The roles the Poet crafted for him now were older men—Lear, Othello, Antony, Macbeth.

It was 1610. The tremor in his hand had become more consistent. His handwriting suffered on occasion, but he kept it to himself the best he knew how. He feared it could be the pox. What years he had left, therefore, he wanted to spend at home, reacquaint himself with his native Warwickshire, walk the high grasses of his boyhood Avon.

Unsure what kind of reception he might get, he did what he could to prepare them. As much as he wanted to, he was careful in his letters not to mention the translation, at least not directly. He did, however, and with modest hyperbole, mention conversations with the King, walking with the King, his plays performed before the King. He wasn't sure what he might salvage with wife Anne, and Judith was Judith. He was never really sure what to expect from either of them. The witty Susanna, however, anticipated his return with great delight. She and husband John visited him often in London. She was particularly fond of the gatehouse at Black Friars. His first letter to her from Richmond didn't say much. Wife Anne could not read, so it allowed him to season his words through his eldest daughter whom he trusted above all others. She was his Rosalind, his Cordelia, his Portia, the hopeful lady that haunted his canon. He wrote her from the Palace.

My harte's Joye,
Your olde father is a wearie of the citie, and longes again for the comfortes and consolacions of home. I do hope to heare from you, and news of children soon, a comfort in my dotage.
Tell mum I am coming home. Tell her I must put my affaires in some order, though I must take thyngs slowly. It may be months yet before I am able to take my leave of London. You will know beste what to say to her and how, my wittie daughter. I hope by the grace of God to be home within ye cominge year. My beste to John. And your sister. I am, always,
Your lovynge father,
Richmond Palace, 19 February 1610.

He was reluctant to be too specific about his arrival, knowing he may have to postpone his trip, but it was a start, a declaration of sorts. Anne may have lost most of her teeth but she still had a healthy bite. With the exception of Susanna, he didn't anticipate a happy homecoming. He would have to buy back the lost years with patience. He could even have grandchildren soon enough if son-in-law John would concentrate. It had been a year and six months since he began his commission. Few issues remained. Most of the work was done, and to the great joy of His Majestie.

The Poet wouldn't admit it, but he deliberately slowed his pace at times, careful to avoid detection. But the King didn't come around as often as he had hoped, and when he did, his visit was brief and the conversation between them strained, or so it seemed to him, as if the King had some business in his mind that vexed him, perhaps some new bout with parliament. It made him uneasy. It seemed to him that whatever royal favor he might have enjoyed was beginning to show signs of fatigue.

The voices within and around him agreed. It was time to go home.

It didn't feel right to him to leave some identifying mark in the King's Bible, however hidden. His role was editorial, not authorial. Whatever influence the scripture may or may not have had on him, in spite of his lost Catholicism and perhaps the guilt associated with his cousin's memory, he had not lived a pious life. Francis meant well, he thought.

THE ISLAND would be his farewell. There, he could leave his identifying mark. It was only right, he thought, that his exit be theatrical. Playwright that he was, he began to orchestrate his departure, and with his usual finesse and prudence. Jonson would notice. And Cecil. Possibly even the King, though his absence would most likely be a relief to a monarch with a secret.

It was the effect his absence would have on Francis he regretted most.

Thinking of Francis reminded him of one of the few passages remaining. Inviting him to Richmond, he pressed the Philosopher for an opinion. It was always about the Greek. Francis Bacon had little use for scripture, other than the curious government it seemed to exercise over men's souls. Francis read the passage. Once again, the octavo and the translator's draft were identical. To the Poet's ear it was just a poorly constructed sentence.

> For we knowe that all things worke for the best vnto them that love God which also are called of purpose.

"Tyndale favors the superlative," Francis said, "though I am not sure why he would. Perhaps it is a spiritual distinction, something he wished to squeeze out of the adjective that just isn't there. None of that would matter to Liam Barlow. He is as petty about the Greek as Bois. Or that bloat Jonson. The correct sense of *agathos* (αγαθος) is *good*." Francis looked at the Greek New Testament at the other end of the table and read the passage. "Here is something else, a preposition, *kata* (κατα), which they seemed to have overlooked, or ignored."

The Poet stood by and was saddened at the view. Here was a rare friendship he was about to abandon. He loved the man. Unaware of the activity in his friend's mind, Bacon gave reason upon reason about grammar, and how "translation is at best an approximation," how it is "inclined to suffer no matter how much caution you apply."

After a few minutes of debate, primarily with himself, Bacon made his suggestions. With a mix of sadness, awe, and submission the Poet made the necessary alterations. The amended text appeared thus:

> And ~~For~~ we knowe that all things worke together for ~~the best~~ good to them that loue God, ~~which also~~ to them who are the called ~~of~~ according to his purpose.

Precision was what mattered to the Philosopher, and execution perhaps. Nothing more. Aesthetics had little to do with it.

"Do you hear that, Francis?" the Poet asked, hearing the music again.

"Hear what?"

"Nothing," the Poet replied.

"Did you consider my suggestion?" Francis asked.

"To be wary of Jonson?"

"Well, that too, I . . ."

"And Cecil?"

"Well, that too, and . . ."

"And Lord Chief Justice Coke?" Bacon knew his poet friend was making sport.

"I have something that might interest you. And you will be guilty of no more than the theft of an article, an iota."

The Poet said nothing. He had seen Francis like this before and understood how persuasive he could be. The irony is curious, but Francis Bacon was able to appreciate the poetic vision of his friend unlike anyone else in the Kingdom, with the exception perhaps of his older brother Anthony, who encouraged Francis to meet the Poet in the first place.

"You have an excellent ear, Francis," the Poet said. "In spite of how you wish to conceal or ignore it."

"And you have philosophy in your verses," replied the Philosopher. "In spite of how you wish to call it something else." They both laughed. It was a manner between them.

"You mentioned an article, a jot?"

"I want to show you something," Bacon said. He opened the translator's draft to the Psalms. "Here it is. That you have already made alterations to this text will make my argument easier to digest, and the stealth less egregious to your conscience."

"Francis, I . . ."

"You have only to rid the psalm of a single word."

"Francis."

"Indulge me."

"A single word?"

"From here to . . . here." To emphasize how innocent the consideration was and how little it would hurt, he pointed to the passage in question with the feather end of a quill pen.

"From there to . . . there?"

"Do you mock me?"

The Poet laughed as he bent over the translator's draft. He had edited the lines from this particular psalm months earlier and was pleased with the outcome, as was the King. He had made only one alteration. He changed the translator's "*a help very easily found in troubles*" to "*a very present help in trouble.*" It was the rhythm he salvaged in the alteration.

"From here to here you say?" the Poet asked. "Cap-à-pie? "

"A single word."

He knew it futile to argue with Francis. He studied the last few lines of the psalm for a single deletion or a phrase to alter in the hope of one less word.

Be stil then, and know that I am God: I will bee exalted among the heathen, I will be exalted in the earth.

He spoke the line out loud but without the adverb.

Be stil ~~then~~, and know that I am God: I will bee exalted among the heathen, I will be exalted in the earth.

In a barely audible voice he repeated the phrase again and again, thrilled in the change.

"A painless excision?" asked a happy Bacon.

"And a fortunate," replied his poet friend. "I might have missed it," he said in a smaller voice.

"Now, my confounded poet friend, I want you to count from the first word in the psalm until you come to this word here . . . *shake*." It was an odd request, but the Poet obeyed.

". . . though the mountains shake," he said quietly, baffled. "I count forty-six."

"Now, from the last word in the psalm, count back forty-six words."

"I beseech thee . . ." he said but with no real conviction. He counted in rapid whispers. At forty-six, he stopped counting. He stopped any movement altogether. A shrunken "oh," was all he could manage.[20]

Francis Bacon was neither a religious nor a mystic, but according to the Poet he had "magnificent reach." Bacon can do anything.

"And without injury to the text," the Philosopher said.

"Or any reckless Hebrew," the Poet happily replied. "There is something else, Francis, though I suspect you have noticed already."

"A reference to the King?"

"*The God of* Iacob *is our refuge,*" the Poet read.

Bacon smiled. "The amendment is subtle, painless, the theft of an adverb. There is justice in the act, and I would know wouldn't I?" he said. "If I remember correctly, you will be how old in April?"

The Poet's answer shook joyfully, with paunch. "You have a diabolical wit, Francis. Cecil is a lamb by comparison. But it's not like you, is it?"

The laughter of Francis Bacon is a particularly fine thing.

"You know me too well, chuck. I confess it was suggested to me," Francis said.

"Suggested?"

The Philosopher smiled. "Royally," he said in reply.

"Now I *am* astonished. But why the need for intercession?"

"I think His Majestie wanted you to have the choice, that you might consider it a command from his mouth. I was the most likely candidate for such a delicate embassy. Nothing is to be said of it, of course. Even to the King."

It was done. All that was left was to inform the King. From there, he didn't know what would happen to the altered manuscript. He assumed it would go directly to Mr. Barker's. Either way, it was out of his power. If he had any regret it was the passage in 1 Kings. It toiled in his ear unlike other ones had, and there was no more time to brood or debate any longer.

> The Lord was not in the wind . . . the earthquake . . . or
> the fire. After the fire a small still voice.

The many large volumes he had studied and sweated over the past eighteen months lay quiet before him. He could not look at them now without a sense of triumph, or perhaps triumph seasoned with loss. Scripture for him had always been about language—the highness, the grand procession. That is not to say he didn't know it well, it just never had much presence in his work except to maim a line or two from it, grace the speech of a king, or fatten an oath.

... after the fire ... after the fire

Proverbs was the book in which he made the fewest alterations. He loved a good proverb, of any kind, as long as it was constructed well and had punch. The proverb depends on punch. He loved punch. Punch informed the speech of many of his characters. And he was good at it. His father used to wax loud, long, and full of punch when he was a child. He was always with his father. The old man was ten feet tall back then.

His thoughts turned on him all of a sudden. He looked out the window. The sky above London was dark, and it was only mid-afternoon. He shook himself and looked at the manuscript before him. He considered how apt it was that Wisdom was female. Lucid, Lady Clarity herself. Other than Hamlet, Sir John Falstaff, and select others of their gender, Mercutio perhaps, the most intelligent, savvy, and subtlest of his characters were always women. Or villains.

Wisedome crieth without, she vttereth her voice in the streets: Shee crieth in the chiefe place of concourse, in the openings of the gates: in the city she vttereth her words, saying, How long, ye simple ones, will ye loue simplicitie? And the scorners delight in their scorning, and fooles hate knowledge? Turne you at my reproofe: behold, I will powre out my spirit vnto you, I will make knowen my wordes vnto you.

There was nothing in the old passage that needed alteration. The entreaty, the gravity, the wounded rhapsody; it could have been Lear out in the rain, or Antony in the pulpit. When his reverie ended, he informed the guard that his work was finished, that he desired audience with Salisbury. He knew it would be hours before he got any response, if he got a response at all that day. The King was at Hampton Court, or so he assumed, and it was likely that Cecil was with him. However long it might take for Cecil to respond, he would remain with the translation until he heard something.

Hardly an hour went by when he heard footsteps in the hall. He knew the sound well. It was the King and Cecil together. He could tell by the rhythm they created when they walked side by side, a *swish-clop-drag-clop-swish-swish* kind of beat that the acoustics in the hallway amplified to his great amusement (which he kept to himself, of course). He would give his Cannibal, his half-fish-half-man the step of a king. He attempted to say the name, but a sudden fit of laughter twisted the letters in his mouth. It came out "Caliban." His pitch animated and he said the name again in its altered state. "Caliban." The change in him was immediate. A light returned to his face.

With another fit of laughter, he thought of something else.

The King and Cecil were just outside the chamber door. It would literally be seconds before they entered. It would not be prudent, he thought, for the King to see him hovering over the manuscript, especially after announcing he had completed the work. He turned quickly to the troubled passage in 1 Kings. He had visited and revisited the passage so many times there was a slight deformity of the page that allowed it to fall open at the exact spot. He read swiftly.

"After the fire . . . after the fire . . ." and there it was. With a few hurried strokes he was finished. He wanted to laugh again but restrained himself. An extraordinary peace came over him. How strange it all seemed.

Once the King and his First Minister were in the room together, they shared a few private words after which Cecil left the room, leaving His Majestie, the Poet, and a single Royal Guard. The Poet demonstrated his reverence. His movement was not sluggish in spite of the impediment of flesh. His Majestie said something private to the guard, upon which the guard left the room, leaving only the King and the Poet. His Majestie noted the light around the Poet and assumed it was due to the completion of the work. The King was cheerful, more so than the Poet had seen him in some time. The manuscript was still open at 1 Kings. His Majestie walked to the edge of the table. Noticing the fresh marks on the page and the altered text, he read the entire passage out loud.

And beholde, the LORD passed by, and a great and strong winde rent the mountaines, and brake into pieces the rockes, before the LORD; but the LORD was not in the wind: and after the wind an earthquake, but the LORD was not in the earthquake. And after the earthquake a fire, but the LORD was not in the fire: and after the fire . . . a ~~small still~~ still small voice.

The words were flawless in his mouth, unlike the usual carnival they made. He turned, smiled, and nodded his head. The plumage on the royal cap waved.

As the King continued to read, the Poet thought of his new-christened Caliban. He listened for cues in the King's diction, the thickness of the tongue, the way some words could not survive the tumble in his mouth, even the small noises the King made intermittently. The King turned toward him once again and smiled. "Master Shakespeare . . . we could not be more pleased."

"Majestie," the Poet said with a second bow, a triumph sullied with discomfort. There had been considerable shrink in his doublet of late. With effort, he resumed uprightness. The King overlooked the spectacle and turned his attention once again to the amended translator's draft. As if the Poet were not there, he began to examine passage after passage. The royal concentration was intense, suggesting a kind of agonized Malvolio. The Poet might have nodded off to sleep were it not for the commotion in his head. That, and the occasional word of praise from the King for a particularly fine thread of altered text.

"Are you content, Master Shakespeare? With the work, of course?"

"Majestie." His approbation, like his brevity, was attractive to the King.

"We will have Salisbury manage from here," the King said. "We will leave you now. Know that you have done us a great and immeasurable service. We are aware of the sacrifice you have made remaining nameless and untrumpeted in this enterprise. But nowhere is there a more grateful monarch than ourself. Farewell. Make yourself available to Salisbury." The Poet said nothing, and the King would not let him bow a third time. As the King passed through the door, without turning back to the Poet he said, "We will advise Mr. Tylney to reopen the playhouses at once." The Poet started to bow. The King waved him off.

 CHAPTER TEN

Like the Old Whore He Was

IF ROBERT CECIL WAS SLITHERING AND METHODICAL, Ben
Jonson was brash and sudden. Even so, the playwright knew it
foolish not to take counsel from the great man. It settled on him
much easier than he expected. He tried to play shy and retiring
at the thought of the murder. It is one thing to imagine his rival's
death, he thought, and even take pleasure from it. It is quite
another to be its author.

Like any performance, the act would demand precision
stagecraft, even as the First Minister suggested. He began to
think of the Poet's murder as he would a play or a masque. It was
easier to think about that way. And what better way for a man of
the theater to make an exit?

He could hardly wait to get to his rooms.

An ego as loud, quarrelsome, and unforgiving as Ben Jonson's could never tolerate a true rival. To consider a dead Shakespeare out of his way at last was all the medication he needed to soothe the injury he felt at the man's very existence.

He felt a sudden reanimation that eased the burden of waiting.

He would be the man who killed William Shakespeare. It would be his contribution to the art he had been so zealous a captain of for years.

Cecil offered him a coach and driver, but in his present state he chose to walk the distance to Shoreditch, just over twenty-miles. The failing light of day would be a boon to his imagination, he thought. He often walked when agitated, particularly at the start of some new enterprise. He didn't mind the distance.

Once home, he began writing, and swiftly, having worked out much of it in his head already. He began to think of his rival in the possessive. "My Shakespeare," he thought to himself. *My* Shakespeare. *Mine*. Who better to do proper justice, he thought, to the great genius of our time? The question both soothed and aggravated in equal doses, but the pieces came together much quicker than he expected.

Soul of an age!

By three the next morning he had written seven pages on the merits of his rival. Afterward, he wasn't sure if he felt better or not.

The applause, delight, the wonder of our stage!

True to the pedagogue's nature, he could not resist the occasional bite, some mild reverie about the Poet's little-Latin-less-Greek shortcomings, but it would all trim, in time, to two pages of useful text.

He was not of an age but for all time!

The hyperbole was so masterful, Jonson knew his name would be remembered with the Poet's, though he wasn't exactly sure what to feel about that either.

Sweet Swan of Avon! A tribute of which he was particularly proud.

With all this rhapsody aimed in the Poet's direction, Jonson began feeding on a whole new proposition, a collection of his own works to be released upon the Poet's death. Delightfully Cecilian, it would redirect attention, making Shakespeare's quiet end quieter. Once he completed this epitaph and prepared his WORKES for publication it would be time to act, the cue to perform his great scene. It was a brilliant plan if he thought so himself, which he had little scruple to do.

He crossed himself and offered a prayer of gratitude on behalf of the lovely, dark, magnificent, lethal, treacherous, grand, and diabolical genius of his patron, Robert Cecil, who would certainly applaud his efforts.

※

He decided to settle the business with Simon Forman as quickly and as quietly as possible. He attributed much of the astrologer's trade to showmanship. But the stage he was accustomed to had rules, and there were no rules for such men. He would get his dram of poison and have nothing more to do with Forman, who was in Cecil's debt for reasons the playwright cared not to speculate. Few men of wit praised or thought of themselves more highly or enthusiastically than Ben Jonson, but even he knew Cecil's mastery of plot to be beyond him.

It was a short walk to Forman's house in Lambeth, less than four miles. Forman had prospered since he had seen him last. The exterior was immaculately groomed, not unlike the home of Dr. Dee in Mortlake. It wasn't an easy thing to unnerve Ben Jonson. He would settle this business with Forman and be on his way. He didn't necessarily need Forman, or Cecil, but he was bound to a specific narrative and there was no undoing it, not without swallowing poison of his own. And he had taken Cecil's gold.

To add to his disquiet, he could not shake the feeling that Forman knew why he was there, that by some devilish art he knew his private intentions, and who they were aimed at. It crept all over the playwright's skin and seemed to smile menacingly upon him. This wasn't completely true, but it hardly mattered. It felt that way to him. Jonson was a shameless self-promoting poet-pedant-playwright, not a mystic.

Simon Forman was cordial, if in an oblique and creeping sort of way.

"I am come from my Lord of Salisbury," the playwright said.

"You are in need of physick, yes?"

Jonson held out the leather purse. A servant stepped out of the shadows, took it from him, and slithered away. Forman then reached into the pocket of his waistcoat, took out a vial, and handed it to the playwright.

"To your better health, Master Jonson," Forman said. "And a quiet mind." Jonson took the vial from him and examined it.

"There is nothing in it."

"Of course, there is. Look closer." The strangeness annoyed Jonson. Against what light there was in the parlor he held the vial to his eyes. As he examined it, he heard a woman's voice in a chamber nearby. He suspected some distress. Forman made no acknowledgement of it.

Again, seeing nothing in the vial and thinking the man to have lost his mind, Jonson said, "I am sorry to have troubled you. I see I have come to the wrong place." He then turned and started to walk away. He suspected it was an exercise in metaphor, which annoyed him even more.

"Justice," the man said. Jonson stopped, then turned and looked at Forman. "Redress. Satisfaction. And from one you call . . . friend." His face flush with new anger, Jonson turned again to leave. "Immediate dispatch may grant thee a moment's satisfaction," the man said as the playwright approached the door. "But so would the dagger or maul. You would hardly need my art." Jonson stopped once again and remained motionless. He felt like a toy for the man's amusement. He heard the same woman's voice groan, and again Forman continued as if nothing were out of the ordinary. Jonson was aware of the man's appetite for strange flesh, his reputation as a seducer of women. "My suggestion is to take what pleasure you will," the man said. Noticing the sudden change of color on the playwright's face, he added, "from a slower, quieter fall I mean."

After a long, unsettling pause, the man spoke again. "Peace, Master Jonson. I make no sport of thee. But my assessment . . . accurate, is it not? I will wager a purse of gold that it is."

Jonson remained expressionless.

"I too am an artist," Forman continued. "I diagnose. I interpret. I recommend and I dispense a specific cure according the nature of the ailment. It is a profound art, I assure you. Your peace, sir, is within my power. So tell me, do you prefer an instant dispatch? Do you wish to witness the spectacle?

What measure of suffering do you prefer, or not? There is much to consider." The questions confounded the playwright. He had thought continually about the bigger picture, the result and the impact of the deed, particularly for its benefit to himself, but he had not considered the actual details. He froze slightly. "Walk with me." Jonson did as he was told and followed the strange man deeper into the bowels of the house as if being led through a labyrinth. He led Jonson into a room he called the *laboratory*. Jonson remembered Dr. Dee had used the word.

"You look surprised," Forman said. "What did you expect, pentacles, boiling cauldrons, drowned babies, 'bladders, and musty seeds, remnant of packthread and old cakes of roses?'"[21]

The reference from the Poet's ROMEO was good-natured provocation, and it succeeded in relieving a noticeable tension. The strange man opened a small drawer and from a glass jar filled the vial with a fine pinkish gray powder. Once sufficiently filled, he handed the vial to the playwright, who studied its contents.

"How do I administer this?"

"With great satisfaction, I am sure."

"May I ask what this vial contains?"

"Liberation," Forman said. Jonson knew he was not going to get a direct answer from Simon Forman any more than he would from Robert Cecil. He also understood the attraction between them. Jonson did not like the man, the tedium of his responses, or his continuing use of metaphor, which he applied with what he considered thuggery and presumption. But it wasn't necessary to like him. "Be resolute," the man said soberly. "Once ingested, there is no escape, no antidote. The first day he will fall into a gloom. The second day, fever will set in. His mind will go into a fume, slowly, taking with it the powers of speech. On the third day the light will go out. Forever."

Jonson took the vial and put it in his pocket. He wanted to suggest that the man leave the poetry to someone else, but he didn't.

"Suffering is not the point," Jonson said. "Just . . . silence."

"Depending on the individual's health at the time, his frame of mind, death will call at a whisper. *Sotto voce.* Slow dispatch will remove suspicion." Questioning him no further and eager to leave that house, Jonson left Forman to his business, unsure exactly what that business was.

Simon Forman was the quintessential multitasker, as many in the occult arts were in those days. But the playwright didn't wish to have his stars analyzed, his handwriting, his cranium, the palms of his hands, the lineaments of his face, his urine, or any other body part, exposed or otherwise. Nor did he care to know the fate of the woman. Cecil would not have recommended the man had he been of doubtful ability, and though Jonson remained wary, he had full confidence in the little vial now in his possession.

"I could consult the stars for the best time to act," Forman said, "give you the certainty you seem to crave." However tempting it sounded, Jonson did not wish to be in the man's power any more than he already was. "One more thing. This powder is of an un-usual potency. It can last for years. It will be ready when you are."

He had no reason not to trust Forman, he just didn't. The more the man pressed Jonson to sample one of his therapies, the more he felt he was being conned. A charlatan, a peddling mountebank, a womanizer of appetite, what little he had heard of the man, he might have made a fine actor.

Being a short distance from Southwark, he made some excuse about rehearsals. Forman knew he was lying and did not protest. Jonson turned to leave, then stopped. Nothing about the house looked the same as it did when he was first led down its corridors. "This way, Master Jonson," the strange man said.

Lambeth to Southwark was a short walk. He thought about visiting an old friend, Cuthbert Burbage, who was using the downtime wisely, making needed repairs on the Globe. Though Jonson often denounced his bricklaying past, he had been friends with the carpenter for many years and appreciated his trade, his manner, the crudeness of his tongue, and, of course, his high regard for Jonson's talent. With his mind abuzz with a grand new production, he thought better of the visit. Before leaving Bankside, however, he turned toward the Stews[22] and his favorite vice, Molly Squires.

He thought about the woman in Forman's house and felt sorry for her whoever she was. He made the sign of the cross as he passed the church of St. Mary Overie.

Jonson had known Molly for years. "As magnificent an old whore as you will find in all the realm," he always added when her name came up. She wasn't much to look at. She had bad teeth, foul breath, and was in her early forties (if he could believe her report), well used and well past her prime. And Jonson could not resist her. Truth is, Molly brought out the "old whore" in Jonson and he loved her for it.

As he approached her dwelling he slowed his stride. He didn't have the brains for it this afternoon, and though brains had precious little to do with a romp in the Stews, he thought better of this too, turned and headed home again. The added tension would be good for his art, he told himself.

On the way home, he allowed his mind to wander. He thought about the events of the past few days, and started considering the entire performance, what Cecil referred to calmly as the "fall of a great house." He began putting elements of the production together in his head, the entire pageant, first to last, adding and subtracting what bits he might as he went along.

When Jonson arrived back in his rooms in Shoreditch, he sat down and began to write. Having successfully put Forman out of his mind, he thought of him again. In an attempt to rid himself of the man he shouted a few obscenities, loudly and in perfect syntax, like the old whore he was. You could hear him from the street below (which the locals ignored). But the more he resisted, the more settled the occult little man remained in his thoughts.

Poised to create as he was, he thought he might make use of the man somehow, and it was certainly much less toil of mind than the death of a rival, which he would need time to orchestrate. So, within the next few hours of intense craft, with the fire of creation burning in his loins and elsewhere, and after a quantity of Sherris sack he had purchased on the way home, he had the beginnings of a new play, one that had nothing at all to do with his rival.

It took him three weeks to write the play, and only a few more to polish it. He took it to Richard Burbage, who took it to the censors for approval. It would turn out to be one of Jonson's more popular plays, which was a relief after the flop of so many other ones. Who would have ever thought the death of a friend could have such a generous effect on his writing?

Just as Cecil predicted, by late spring 1610, the playhouses were in full operation. Theatre queues bulged once again. Plague was rampant. Then it was not. No one questioned the long delay.

Upon the Poet's return to the theater—the routine, the rapid movement, the hum of preparation, the general busyness, even the moments of glory—how dull it seemed to him anymore. He knew better than to try to fight the sensation, and he was never that good of an actor. His first role upon returning to the stage was in a new play by Ben Jonson, THE ALCHEMIST.

The Poet's own play he renamed THE TEMPEST, the first performance of which was on Hallowmas, 1 November 1611, at the palace at Whitehall.

Ben Jonson was doubtless the Poet's best audience, and because he now considered THE TEMPEST to be the Poet's last play, he leaned in closer. After CYMBELINE, which Jonson particularly despised for many reasons, including the acting, he figured Shakespeare was due for something special. To his delight, the central figure in the play happened to be a sorcerer, one who studied the dark arts, who influenced life around him with a blend of magic and wordcraft. Unknown to anyone but him, he took an even greater delight realizing that Shakespeare, like his own Hamlet, was now bound in a play within a play, with only one possible outcome.

In spite of the depth of attention he paid to this first performance, Jonson thought the play "flaccid" (a new French word floating about that he was certain he could make use of),

stitched together with props from former successes. There were
moments, however, that he listened with quiet fascination.

Our revels now are ended. These our actors,
As I foretold you, were all spirits and
Are melted into air, into thin air:
And, like the baseless fabric of this vision,
The cloud-capp'd towers, the gorgeous palaces,
The solemn temples, the great globe itself,
Ye all which it inherit, shall dissolve
And, like this insubstantial pageant faded,
Leave not a rack behind. We are such stuff
As dreams are made on, and our little life
Is rounded with a sleep.

Judged a fine play by many, THE TEMPEST lacked the sparkle of his former efforts and Shakespeare knew it. His next
two plays, THE TWO NOBLE KINSMEN and HENRY VIII, written out of obligation and with an underling, John Fletcher,
had little at all of the old fire. His mind, heart, and genius
were elsewhere.

As poets do, they imagine well, and he imagined excuse after
excuse to stay one more month, two more months, and so on
until another year passed, then another. Finally, in 1613, during
a performance of HENRY VIII, the thatched roof of the Globe
was set on fire by a cannon shot from the stage. The wadding
went afoul, or so it is told. In less than two hours, all that was
left were ashes and a few smoldering boards. There were no ca-
sualties. One man's britches caught on fire, but he had the good
sense to douse the flame with a cup of ale.

Staring at the ashes, the Poet needed no further convincing. It was time to turn homeward, the small voice said. Conditions outstanding, which included the promise of more plays, Burbage reluctantly agreed to let his chief poet retire in peace.

He had made his fortune.

He had cleared and titled his father's name.

His greatest character he named after his dead child, never to be forgotten.

He still didn't know what to think about the tremors in his hand, but he had lost none of his primary faculties, and his handwriting had never been that good anyway.

As delighted, and just as often doubtful as Jonson was about the Poet's assumed retirement, he continued to keep an eye on him. His resolve remained firm. He watched with a kind of wonder as it all unfolded, but made no move. Under Cecil he had learned how to wait, and found great satisfaction in doing so.

Robert Cecil died in 1612. He was worn out. With his death, Jonson was free to do as he wished concerning the Poet, but he had gotten attached to the idea of his decease and had been paid handsomely by his patron. Plus, the little drama had unfolded with such theatrical precision, he felt obliged to keep to script. As a seasoned playwright he would know when the time was right. All he needed to exercise was patience. It would come together under its own power. He would not allow anyone else the murder either, which was his obligation alone. He became jealous over the act, and rehearsed it in his head over and over to perfection. He even began, in his own way, to insure the safety of William Shakespeare, as a butcher might be jealous over a prize lamb. He kept the vial of pink gray powder with him most of the time.

He suspected the Poet's involvement in the King's new Bible, especially with the absence of any masque. But it no longer mattered. There was some mild fanfare upon its release in 1611, the year of THE TEMPEST, but it didn't make the large splash the King anticipated, which delighted Jonson. There was no mention of William Shakespeare in connection with the great work. Most everyone continued to read and enjoy the Geneva Bible.

In the fall of 1613, the Poet left London for Stratford-Upon-Avon.

He didn't know it would be the last time he would see his old friend when they met at the Crown Inn on his way home. Their lives had asked different things of them. Burdened with debt as he was, Bacon was finally getting the royal attention he had always deserved. He cultivated that favor, as anyone might expect, which meant he had less time for his poet friend.

The Poet had prepared Francis for months, or meant to, but every time he spoke of it, either the conviction melted away or Bacon wittingly diverted the conversation altogether. As the newly appointed Attorney General, the King kept Francis Bacon very busy. Still, in spite of his growing distractions of government, the Philosopher didn't want the Poet to leave London. He argued continually, warmly, and persuasively. The Philosopher was never convinced the Poet would leave anyway.

"I don't think so, Francis."

"Of course you will. If just to aggravate that churl Jonson.

He wants nothing more than your absence." The Poet wasn't sure what Jonson had to do with anything but he humored his friend.

"Ben's loud. He loves to hear himself crow."

Bacon shuddered with uneasiness that his friend was so naïve, so young in ways, so old in others, so trusting of a man who cares for no one and no work, no achievement but his own. He had watched Jonson from a safe distance and suspected his attraction to the Poet to have something in it more than gentlemen rivalry, though he could prove nothing.

"He is more pulpiteer than playwright," the Philosopher said. "His greatest sermon is himself, about whom he bleats louder and more continuously than any goat in all of Christendom. He and Cecil are . . . *were*, God bless all Christian souls, close. I can't help but feel some . . ."

"Patronage, Francis. That is . . . *was* the sum of it. And Cecil is dead."

"But Jonson is not. Cecil's habit all his life was to have dangerous men in his power." He let the words fall softly, and said no more about Cecil, Jonson, or the nagging alarm he felt. "Where are you going to be without the noise, the push . . . the applause? The stage is your mistress, Will, your best bed." The Poet laughed. The Philosopher continued. "You're going home to a role you have no talent for. You will grow fat."

"I'm already fat. And nearly bald. I will visit oft enough. The gatehouse at Black Friars is mine now. Come, Francis, let us be merry. On the morrow, I depart for home."

The two men continued in this fashion, the Philosopher arguing why his friend should stay, and the Poet arguing why it was necessary for him to leave. Distracted with the obligations of his new office, the Philosopher knew his words lacked the old heart, as did the Poet. They spent the remainder of the evening together, joined at times by the intoxicating Jennet Davenant.

"Then tell me one thing."

"Anything, chuck."

"For the satisfaction of a curiosity. Your complaint with Southampton."

The Poet laughed. "Call it a . . . territorial dispute," he said.

"Properties?"

The Poet said nothing.

"A woman?"

The Poet still said nothing.

"A boy?"

The Poet laughed again. "Emilia," he said.

"Emilia?"

"Lanyer."

"The singer?"

"The rhapsody in my blood," the Poet said.

"And to that quack Forman," the Philosopher said under his breath.

"Did you say 'that black woman?'"

"She *is* Venetian, a Moor."

"Amour, indeed," the Poet said. "My sun warmed olive. I introduced her to my Lord of Southampton."

"A grave error in judgment, my duck."

"I visited the good Earl one sunny afternoon."

"And the good Earl was not expecting you."

"A serving man tried to tell me he was at a play."

"But he prevaricated," the Philosopher said. "For the peacock was not at a play."

"No, but he was in character."

"I'm sure he was. And just what character was he in?" The Poet laughed and let the jest bloom where planted. "He was . . ." the Philosopher tried to continue.

"Don't say it," the Poet interrupted.

"I have it!"

"He was decked in woman's weeds," the Poet interjected. "Flowing mane, white face, a pretty leg, a cherry lip."

"This is hardly news."

"It was to me. And my bronze Emilia? In the Earl's doublet, hose, and cap."

"That's it? That's the quarrel between you and the Earl that so confounded Cecil?"

"I took it out on a sonnet."

"I would hope so. There is no chastisement quite like your pentameter. You should punish the dark lady," the Philosopher said. "Emilia too, for that matter." His laughter wheezed.

"For I have sworn thee fair and thought thee bright, who art as black as hell, as dark as night."[23]

"There's a hardy wound."

"The slander?"

"Thy rhyme."

"The King appointed Southampton as factor for my fee."[24]

"Grant ye, that wasn't easy for the Earl to swallow," the Philosopher said, to the Poet's scandaling smile. "I've been with them often, together, Southampton and the King. Insufferable."

"As a pair of queens?" the Poet added.

It was the old laughter. The two men spoke on this wise until daybreak. The Philosopher warned him again about Jonson, though he doubted it left an impression.

The Poet departed for Stratford that same afternoon.

I Ridde My Soule
of Thee at Laste

"TO SPIT OR FART FIRE!"[25] There was no mistaking the voice, or the text. The Poet turned in his stool, amazed to see the bearlike figure of his old friend at the entrance of the tavern. He thought nothing of the sudden chill at the back of his neck. The night air, he said to himself.

But his bearlike friend had been patient long enough. It was 1616. THE WORKES OF BENJAMIN JONSON was ready for publication. The Poet's name was in decline. The stars were charitable. It was time to act.

Jonson had given himself a week to get to Stratford, just over a hundred miles, and was in no rush. Seven days to rehearse the action, every entrance and exit. Seven days to polish every move, to con every speech. He left Shoreditch Sunday, 14 April 1616, and arrived at Stratford-Upon-Avon Saturday, 20 April.

The day was cold, with a bite. Beautiful, in its way, but unseasonable, April in name but not spirit, in thought but not intention, more the ghost of April than April. The Avon was in flood following heavy rains. Since the Poet was born on 23 April, Jonson hoped to time his performance, that his rival might expire on the same day. It was art. It was also a concession. He owed the Poet that much. Or that was the fiction as he understood it. Being born and dying on the same day carries a scent of the inauthentic, and Jonson knew that.

It didn't take him long to find The Thatch, the only drinking establishment in the one-tavern town. It was Saturday night. He didn't expect the Poet to be alone, but he didn't expect to see Michael Drayton, another Warwickshire poet of some renown. The two poets were steeped in drink by the time Jonson arrived. He thought it an apt beginning to his little production.

"O happy hour!" the Poet cried. Jonson took a seat at table with the two poets.

"Ben," Drayton said dryly, with little, if any, animation.

"More sack, Francis!" Jonson said. Loudly. They actually were drinking sack, and the drawer's name actually was Francis, but Drayton thought the lump playwright's rendition a bit flat.

"What brings you here, Ben?" the Poet asked.

"There is so little sport in your absence, Will. And a murther of young crows has infested the city. I thought I would surprise you, ply thee with drink."

"I would thou hang thyself," Drayton said in a quiet voice.

"What's that?"

"I thought the same thing myself," Drayton answered.

"More sack!" the Poet said in a loud voice.

"And to give you this," Jonson added. He held what appeared to be a small letter, folded and sealed.

"A poem?" asked the Poet with a slight lift in his voice, reaching for the letter. "A sonnet perhaps?" Jonson brushed the Poet's hand out of the way and tucked the letter in the pocket of his jerkin.

"Later," Jonson insisted. Nothing more was said of it.

Drayton respected Jonson but didn't like him. He thought him loud. He didn't sense any present alarm, though he thought Jonson's great goodwill overplayed.

"You have traveled a long way to see a friend," Drayton observed.

"Nonsense! And what is it to you if I have missed the little bastard?" All three poets laughed. The Poet had gained even more weight since Jonson had seen him last. He didn't look well. The idleness, he thought. Or the wife.

A young drawer brought the three of them another round of the Sherris sack. "The pitcher," Jonson snapped. "Leave it." Upon taking a deep draught, he said very loudly, and in character, "If I had a thousand sons, the first humane principle I would teach them should be to forswear thin potations and to addict themselves to sack."[26]

Even Drayton laughed at Jonson's Falstaff, having always suspected the Poet used Jonson as a model, at least in part, for the mouthy bawd.

And so went the evening.

They drank. They argued Ovid and Holinshed. They drank some more. They argued Foxe, the Poet's "bungling" of Julius Caesar, and how Donne deserved hanging. They drank even more and laughed about the King's latest folly with his lovely George.[27] Their exchanges had little of the old fire of their London tavern bouts. Drayton had heard much of it before and doused his tedium with drink.

Though dull by London standards, The Thatch kept a steady crowd of Stratford regulars. And though the name Shakespeare had grown, he remained the friendly alien among them, preferring a quiet celebrity.

Later in the evening, the Poet begged leave that he might step outside and relieve himself. Drayton, not wanting to be left alone with Jonson, asked to accompany him that he might obey the call of his own nagging bladder. As the two men walked toward the entrance of the tavern, Jonson laughed to himself with a private amusement.

The spotlight is now on him.

With little fuss and drawing no attention to himself, he reached into the pocket of his waistcoat and took out the little vial. O vile, indeed. He had no scruples, nor did he expect to be bothered by any. He thought of Cecil, how precise he had been concerning cool vengeance. He thought of Forman (then shook him off). He tapped the vial with his index finger to loosen the powder, then quickly, cautiously, as he had dreamed of and rehearsed often, emptied the contents into the Poet's cup.

He looked longingly at Drayton's cup, but the vial was empty.

Both poets returned, and at a slower pace than they had walked out. Once they were at the table, Jonson took the pitcher and topped off their cups. He took the Poet's cup and handed it to him, swilling it about as he did.

"My good lads, my good lads," he said in a pleasant voice, deflecting any opportunity for protest. He stood, lifted his cup, looked at his old friend, and said, "To the chief musician." After a generous pause, he continued. "Our gentle Shakespeare, my . . . Shakespeare, my elder in the faith, the likes of which England has never known . . . nor will ever know again." Having rehearsed the tribute, it bore a grace of sincerity that moved even Drayton.

"Please, Ben," the Poet protested. "Not one drop more."

"Nonsense," the playwright answered.

"Let us then drink to this life we've been given," the Poet said soberly, or as soberly as he was able. "Ben . . . Michael."

"I rid my soul of thee at last," is what Jonson wanted to say, what he had prepared in his head, but he kept the benediction to himself.

"Let us drink deep," Drayton added.

"Cup and all," Jonson answered as his old friend and rival drank down the draught to its dregs. The two Warwickshire poets were far too inebriated to detect any sudden pang of conscience, had there been any.

But it was done. The rest depended on the accuracy of Simon Forman.

The night ended and the three men went their own way.

"Stay with us tonight, Ben," said the Poet, "at New Place."

"I have a room at The Howard."

"Tomorrow then. Let us dine together," the Poet said. His words warm, drunken.

"Tomorrow," said Jonson.

The Poet walked away with a noticeable alteration to his gait. "And tomorrow," he said, adding a jubilant, "Adieu."

In his rooms later that night, staring into a fire, still under the spell of the Sherris and his grand performance, Jonson tried to muster a tear but could not.

The next day, as anticipated, the Poet fell into a gloom.

Michael Drayton left that morning for London. Jonson was gone by then.

By the next afternoon a fever came on the Poet. John Hall, his son-in-law, was summoned. He suspected typhus and demanded seclusion, though, in truth, he knew his diagnosis a poor one. As Forman predicted, the Poet died the third day, 23 April 1616. *Sotto voce.*

Susanna, riffling tearfully and heatedly through her father's effects, found the folded paper in the pocket of his jerkin. She broke the seal, opened it, and read it quietly. It sounded like her father. Or it may have. She wasn't sure. There was no name fixed to it and it was written in a much neater hand. She didn't know what to think and debated in her heart why he might have written such a thing, if he wrote it at all. She was studying the lines when her mother appeared, who demanded she read it to her.

Anne, the Shrew, said the verse would make a suitable ornament to his grave. It was one less thing she would have to think about. In spite of the uncertainty of its authorship, it was not possible for Susanna to read the words without a quiver of sorrow on her lips. But she did as her mother asked.

Good friend for Jesus sake forbear,
To dig the dust enclosed here.
Blessed be the man that spares these stones,
And cursed be he that moves my bones.

English piety and superstition being what it was in 1616, and with the observance of a curse, the Poet's bones never left Holy Trinity in Stratford, where they remain undisturbed to this day. More importantly, they would never rest at Poet's Corner [Westminster Abbey] beside Chaucer, Spenser, Michael Drayton. Or Ben Jonson.

Though it seemed to dissipate as quietly and as quickly as it spread, speculation flooded gossip streams from Stratford to London and elsewhere, including an account by a Reverend Davies, a vicar from Stratford-Upon-Avon, who reported with some indifference that in his best opinion the Poet died of what amounted to a severe bout of dyspepsia, having eaten too many pickled herrings and drinking too much Canary wine (which, in truth, was Sherris sack). No foul play was suspected.

THE WORKES OF BENJAMIN JONSON was released one month after the Poet's death. Jonson paid for a grand celebration in his own honor. Later that same year, King James issued a warrant that outlawed the Geneva Bible, still the most popular translation in England.

The Author

David Teems is the best-selling author of MAJESTIE: THE KING BEHIND THE KING JAMES BIBLE (Thomas Nelson/Harper Collins, 2010), and TYNDALE: THE MAN WHO GAVE GOD AN ENGLISH VOICE (Thomas Nelson/Harper Collins, 2012). In 2017, David was a presenter on the National Geographic series, ORIGINS: THE JOURNEY OF MANKIND as an expert on the life and influence of William Tyndale.

David and his wife, Benita, live in Franklin, Tennessee, near their sons Adam and Shad, with their wives Katie and Robin. David and Benita have five grandchildren, ages range from one to fifteen years.

Endnotes

1   ANTONY AND CLEOPATRA, 1.4.4-7.

2   ANTONY AND CLEOPATRA, 2.2.195-209.

3   HAMLET, 3.2.160-161.

4   HAMLET, 3.2.165-168.

5   HAMLET, 5.2.345.

6   *God said, "Let there be light," and there was light.* Genesis 1:3.

7   Ben Jonson was found guilty of killing Gabriel Spenser in a duel on 22 September 1598. He pleaded *benefit of clergy* (essentially, he could read) and was released. His left thumb was branded with the letter T, for Tyburn, the place of execution where he would be hanged upon any second offense.

8   HENRY IV, PART ONE, 2.4.492-498.

9   *Fu gia in Venezia un Moro*—"There was a Moor in Venice." Opening of Geraldi Cinthio's HECATOMMITHI, the chief source for OTHELLO.

10 HENRY IV, PART TWO, 3.1.30-31.

11 *"More matter, with less art."* HAMLET, 2.2.95.

12 MACBETH is also known as The Scottish Play.

13 Iacobus Rex. James king.

14 SONNET 101.6-7.

15 *octavo*—a small book, "traditionally produced by folding a standard printing sheet three times to form a section of eight leaves; a book with pages of this size (in earlier uses, sometimes with the implication of popular appeal or cheapness); a page or piece of

paper of this size. (*in* octavo—with leaves one-eighth of a standard printing sheet in size; in an edition having leaves of this size.) Other sizes include *folio*, a full-sized sheet folded once, and *quarto*, a sheet folded twice. *The Oxford English Dictionary.*

16 A MIDSUMMER NIGHT'S DREAM, 5.1.7-17.

17 RICHARD II, 3.2.27-28.

18 *All the world's a stage.* [Latin, literally, "all the world is an actor."]

19 MACBETH, 5.3.22-23.

20 One of the oldest mysteries in the Shakespeare imaginary, in the 1611 version of the King James Bible, starting at the first word in Psalm 46 (not counting the introductory attribution) and counting forty-six words you come to the word *shake*. Counting backward forty-six words (not including *Selah*) you come to the word *spear*.

21 ROMEO AND JULIET, 5.1.46-47.

22 The Stews were licensed brothels in and around Southwark.

23 SONNET 147.13-14.

24 "There is one instance so singular in its magnificence of this patron of Shakespeare's that if I had not been assured that the story was handed down by Sir William D'Avenant, who was probably very well acquainted with his affairs, I should not venture to have inserted; that my Lord Southampton at one time gave him a thousand pounds to enable him to go through with a purchase which he heard he had a mind to. A bounty very great and very rare at any time, and almost equal to that profuse generosity the present age has shown to French dancers and Italian eunuchs."—Nicholas Rowe, SOME ACCOUNT OF THE LIFE OF WILLIAM SHAKESPEAR, 1709.

25 Ben Jonson, A MASQUE OF THE METAMORPHOSED GYPSIES.

26 Line spoken by Sir John Falstaff in Henry IV, Part Two [4.3.132-135] by William Shakespeare.

27 George Villiers (1592-1628), 1ˢᵗ Duke of Buckingham (created by James) became the new "favourite" of King James in 1614, replacing the Scot and less fortunate Robert Carr. James showed little discretion where George was concerned. To parliament the King once said, "Christ had John, and I have George."